THE DIVINITY GENE

MATTHEW J. TRAFFORD

The

DIVINITY GENE

STORIES

Douglas & McIntyre

D&M PUBLISHERS INC.

Vancouver/Toronto/Berkeley

Douglas & McIntyre
An imprint of D&M Publishers Inc.
2323 Quebec Street, Suite 201
Vancouver BC Canada V5T 4S7
www.douglas-mcintyre.com

Cataloguing data available from Library and Archives Canada
ISBN 978-1-55365-603-6 (pbk.)
ISBN 978-1-55365-636-4 (ebook)

Editing by Barbara Berson
Cover and text design by Jessica Sullivan
Cover illustrations by Jessica Sullivan
Printed and bound in Canada by Friesens
Text printed on acid-free, 100% post-consumer paper
Distributed in the U.S. by Publishers Group West

We gratefully acknowledge the financial support of the Canada Council
for the Arts, the British Columbia Arts Council, the Province of British
Columbia through the Book Publishing Tax Credit, and the Government
of Canada through the Canada Book Fund for our publishing activities.

MIX
Paper
FSC FSC® C016245

FOR MY FAMILY:

Michele Frances Trafford, my reading mother
Larry James Trafford, athlete and scholar
& Thomas Andrew Trafford, my bromo

TABLE OF CONTENTS

THORACIC EXAM

The patient's name is Kennedy Slippington. She sits before me on the table wearing a standard hospital-issue gown. Ms. Slippington, brunette, has her hair pulled up away from her neck and shoulders. She looks to me like the type of woman who, upon entering middle age, is careful to have all the most thorough medical examinations as a preventative measure against disease, a self-care practice that as a nurse I admire and promote. I check her file and see that she has not presented with any unusual pain or respiratory distress and is not taking medication—facts I check with her verbally to make certain.

Unsurprisingly, she is a non-smoker and exercises regularly. It has been a year since her last in-depth thoracic exam. I ask her to lower her gown to the waist, and I begin.

There are many things most people don't know about the lungs. That the apex of each lung, for example, extends slightly above the clavicle. That the base of each lung sits far higher than is generally thought—at the tenth rib, about halfway down the back. Many nurses who have not kept up their training end up auscultating much lower than they should, in effect listening to the diaphragm or viscera. Many nurses also neglect the lateral portion of the examination, which yields important access to the right middle lobe. I have recently upgraded my credentials in con-ed college classes at night.

I decide to perform the tests involving the stethoscope first, because I know it is at room temperature and I fear my fingers may still be cold from going outside at lunch. I do not wish to make her uncomfortable. I explain what I am about to do. I ask her to repeat either "ninety-nine" or "blue moon," the standard two phrases set by medical practitioners to create measurable resonance.

"Blue moon," she says, as I move the stethoscope along its prescribed path, left side, right side, right side, left, checking for the proper bronchophony. "Blue moon. Blue moon." And then she sobs so violently it hurts my ears and the lurch of her diaphragm is visible to the naked eye.

"I'm sorry," she articulates, "I'm so sorry." She brings her hands to her face quickly, then seems to change her mind and starts wiping her eyes and inspiring her mucus loudly. "My husband . . . he died recently. He . . . he used to jump out of planes. You know, skydive, as a hobby. I never liked him to do it, but he was stubborn. Oh, was he ever." She bangs her hands on the table, then brings them to her face again, then lowers them to her lap and looks up at me. "His parachute failed to open during his last jump. He was in Vermont. All I got was a phone call: *Are you Mrs. Noah Michael Kunst?* They had to ship the body—and—and now that's it, there's just nothing. No investigation, no liability, no *reason*. He's just gone, and it's something I'm supposed to just accept. That this type of accident happens all the time." Her lacrimal ducts are now secreting full tears, and I can hear by her voice that her sinuses have started to fill. "I'm sorry," she says again, "I'm sorry. I don't usually break down like this."

In front of her, my stomach has filled with liquid ether and my knees are trembling so hard I have grabbed the table for support.

This isn't sympathy.

FOR WITH THE sound of that name I am nineteen again in Prague, city of a thousand spires, unspoiled by war and flaunting a gorgeous tapestry of paradox: old and new, Byzantine and Renaissance, atheist and Hussite and Catholic and Jewish, communist and nascent capitalist, subterranean and alpine. At this age I still believe art matters, am still content to spend my time wrangling with colour and line and form, or clumsily cobbling words together to make poems, sitting in countless underground bars illuminated solely by the glow of Pilsner beer and men's smiles, wearing black and discussing Truth or Politics while smoking vanilla-scented tobacco from South American countries, crossing and uncrossing my legs and trying always to appear witty, fey, or beautiful.

I couldn't get enough of life back then: strawberries exploded in my mouth with the sweet prick of love and possibility, I drank wine by the bottle and dipped dense dumplings in goulash twice a day, took an assortment of men to my bed with abandon and true revelling in the joy of my own body, until I met Noah. Noah, whom everyone had mentioned as either a hero or a rogue, who had been there since the Curtain fell, who now ran the prominent English newspaper and pursued serious journalism, and whom I finally met at a reading in December when the cobblestones

Thoracic Exam

were covered with snow that glistened in the headlights of trams trundling through the night. Noah, who repeatedly ran fingers through his dark hair when nervous, whose dimple was shy and unpredictable, who always looked mischievous. Noah, who warned me about his native Missouri and any state with a boot-heel or a panhandle, and who debated with me for hours about the pronunciation of "wabe" in the Jabberwocky poem. Noah, who once told me about his unbridled passion for collage, manically cutting bits from magazines and newspapers and tourist brochures and pasting together mosaics of high-gloss irony and full-colour satiric bite, whose early poems in the now defunct literary magazines were superlative and had the mark of the farm boy he once was—cows, rattlesnakes, barns—and who would come out to cavernous music clubs only to sit and resist the beat, who only danced once, at his best friend's birthday party, joining us and swaying with his hands on his pelvis, holding them up and angled inwards like a háček, almost crude, who excited me and paralyzed me and who never ever made the first move.

Who once shared with me three small bottles of Becherovka, that golden Czech liqueur that tastes of Christmas, distilled from pine needles and smelling almost of cinnamon, as he slowly unbuttoned his shirt and tried on the ridiculous straw hats we'd bought in the flea markets near the Florenc bus station, and we took our shoes off and rubbed each other's feet, and I dared to ask about his tattoo: a crescent moon, tattooed in cornflower blue above his left nipple. Like him it was gorgeous but seemed unfinished somehow—a little too pale, a slight waver in the lines—and he had the air of a man disclosing a deep secret, or else I willfully mistook regret for confessional intimacy, while he told me: "I was really drunk one night in college—they're not supposed to give you tattoos when you're drunk. Across the street there was some insurance company, and this was their logo. I just looked out the window and told the guy to put it on my chest." I wanted to ask if he was wearing a shirt when he walked into the parlour, because to me it seemed like the most important detail, the detail that would lead to tracing the tattoo with the tip of my tongue, grazing his nipple with my teeth, kissing the hollow of his breastbone and letting gravity and drunkenness and sheer desire pull my mouth lower and lower, but I collapsed into giggles or hiccoughs or vomiting or else I simply passed out before I could.

Noah, who one winter night, drunk and warm with good food and a glow of superiority, walked me home from a poetry reading at Shakespeare and Sons, down Krymská and through the narrow streets, with snowflakes the size of saucers falling on his navy pea coat, catching in his hair, on his eyelashes, and in front of my doorway leaned in and kissed me, his thin moist lips pressing against my fuller ones for three hard seconds, until he pulled away with a pleased look on his face, and instead of following me inside said "Have a good night, kid" and got into a taxi and left.

Who was the reason I left Prague defeated, because he never even alluded to that kiss again nor paid enough attention to me to satisfy, because I could never ask him why he turned away or tell him how desperately I wanted him, because I hated myself for that and hated him for not seeing it and loving me or wanting me or, at the very, very least, offering me an explanation of why not.

"MS. SLIPPINGTON," I say, "please pull yourself together."

I coil the stethoscope and lay it on the counter. I take a deep breath, and turn back to her.

Thoracic Exam

I continue the exam by rote, my fingers moving like mechanized rods. I palpate the skin, checking for lumps, bumps, lesions, discoloration, cyanosis. What I long to see now are the puckered scars of cigarette burns, raised welts, bruising; some sign her life has included trauma, chronic pain. I want to see proof that Noah abused her, that having him was poisonous to her. Or else I want to find evidence of why she was more worthy of him than I was. Yet everything about her remains standard. Her costal angle is exactly ninety degrees.

I begin to auscultate her anterior thorax. The first two fingers of my left hand against her chest, then a quick rap on the first knuckles with the index finger of my right, a little harder than I should. First position. Second. I locate the angle of Louis.

I ask her to raise and separate her breasts, and auscultate between them on either side of the sternum. My fingers leave round white impressions that fade instantly when I move my fingers away. Her skin is dry, and I wonder how often he licked her sweat from this place, or from her suprasternal notch. I wonder if she ever held her breasts like this while he fucked her from behind. I put my hand on her wrist to show she can let go.

I move to her posterior thorax. I place my hand gently on her head and angle it forward. At the nape of her neck the bone rises beneath the skin, c7, the *vertebra prominens*. I can see how he would have bent his head and kissed her here. I want to place my lips around this bone, feel its contours between my teeth, puncture the flawless skin. If I were to slice her in this place she would be wheelchair-bound for life. There are scalpels less than three feet away.

Instead I auscultate her back, desperate to find something unusual, anything. I imagine a raised mole with suspicious edges, or an adipose cyst. I imagine his name tattooed above her left kidney, or a blue crescent moon to match his under her shoulder blade. She is maddeningly blank. Worse, I can find no sign of him. I want to touch him again in some small way, want her body to bring his back to me.

At my behest she places her hands on her head, so I can examine her laterally. I think immediately of handcuffs and girdles. Noah hog-tied beneath a whip-wielding Ms. Slippington. His tongue gliding across her black patent-leather boot. I picture him watching her from bed as she ties her hair up each morning, takes it down each night before coming to join him.

I snatch up the stethoscope again, not because it's required but because I must eavesdrop inside of her. I am no longer assessing normal breath sounds, bronchial or vesicular, or checking for wheezing or crackles in the peripheral lobes. I'm just listening to this woman breathe in and out, inflation and deflation of pink alveoli, closing my eyes and hearing the air rush in and out of her body, knowing that Noah has breathed in unison with this woman, shared breath with her and been inside her.

Finally, I perform a diaphragmatic excursion exam, a difficult test most nurses omit through ignorance or lack of skill. I am being very, very thorough. This is Noah's wife. She has gained and lost what I never came close to. Everything about her is normal.

"I'm finished," I say. "You can put your robe back on." She complies as I pick up her chart again and uncap my pen. I press hard when I sign my name and go over and over my signature until I am afraid the paper will tear. I arrange my face into a professional expression of sympathy and concern.

"I hate to be the bearer of bad news, but there is a problem with your right lung. I'm hearing adventitious and abnormal

Thoracic Exam

breathing sounds with decreased airflow, and the responses there are dull instead of resonant. I can't tell you anything for certain, of course, but these symptoms are usually indicative of a growth in the lungs, in your case a rather substantive mass of tissue. I'll notify your physician immediately, and he'll follow up with you to arrange for further testing, an x-ray, and a biopsy and whatever else may be deemed necessary."

Kennedy Slippington looks at me with dilated pupils, her face paler now than when we started. Her eyebrows have knit together, as though she is concentrating very intently on a mental task, recognizing a forgotten scent, translating awkward phrases from a foreign language. Her jaw is slack so that her mouth hangs open, revealing her perfect teeth. "Oh my God," she whispers. "Oh my." And then, extremely softly, "Thank you for telling me."

I hold her gaze for three seconds, then turn from her; my heart rate accelerates and my chest constricts. This is the first time I have turned my back on a patient in distress, knowingly hurt someone. There will probably be consequences. But then again, hospitals are large and crowded places. This type of accident happens all the time.

PAST PERFECT

Dylan wandered away while the sale was still in progress; he knew that Princeton's two friends—the ones with shiny hairless shins and ebullient white chest hair and interchangeable names—that those old friends of Princeton's from long before Dylan's time would look after the running of the sale until he got back. He was walking east on the north side of Maitland, his own little corner of the world, and feeling sick about his neighbours—the ones in the building and the ones who lived nearby—who all looked at him now with sympathy and pity and a tinge of fear. They made him sick because they thought they knew what had happened to Princeton, why he'd gotten rapidly thinner and weaker and more sallow, why he'd stopped going out, why he was bedridden now, refusing visitors, why Dylan was selling all of Princeton's things: selling his treasured vinyl records, the Blossom Dearie and the Bach and the Neil Young; the 1920s vintage clothing and celebrity memorabilia of James Dean and Rock Hudson and many others; the meticulously restored antique deacon's benches and dowry chests; his Royal Doulton china, complete sets of

Tennyson and Lichfield, the odd Albany handled cake plate here and Biltmore rimmed soup bowl there; his Val Saint Lambert crystal champagne bucket; his Victorian dolls and Bunnykins and Beswick miniatures and porcelain replicas and Wolfard blown glass; his first edition of Rudyard Kipling's *Captains Courageous* and all the other rare books; all of it. Dylan knew the assumptions people made about Princeton, saw their *schadenfreude* stares and saw them darting in like magpies around his husband's glittering possessions, and his reaction was to feel sick and walk away.

He turned south onto Church at the Super Freshmart, run by a Korean family, and waved at Glen sitting on his milk crate in front of the store, his hat filled with change warm from the pockets of the men strolling by, Glen holding a stick with a string attached, as though fishing for money in his own hat. Dylan had talked to him, so knew that he was unemployed, not homeless. He also knew if people would only ask *him* he would tell them that Princeton had brain cancer, not AIDS. But he realized how hard it could be to ask a simple question.

He thought about how quickly things can change, walking past O'Grady's which used to be Wilde Oscars, alive with the chatter of people whose husbands weren't dying as they dined on the patio, past Play, which used to be something else he couldn't remember, past the Bank of Montreal, which used to be an American Apparel and before that was Body Body Wear, past all the new and remembered bars he frequented when he was single.

He walked down Church towards Carlton, noticing for the first time the new street signs that said Church-Wellesley Village and had a rainbow on them, wondering when those had gone up. He let people look at him and acknowledged the occasional whistle with a smile but no eye contact. It was a Saturday, one of those first really warm weekends, when the patios spring open and are packed by ten AM, and the giggling twinks with fresh faux-hawks venture downtown from the suburbs for the first time since winter, and all the muscle marys in tank tops and cut-off denim shorts and the queens in polo shirts and khakis with little yipping dogs all parade themselves up and down Church Street, preening and primping and generally flaunting it. And Dylan knew all they would see in him was his jeans and sandals and shoulder bag, eye candy, a hot young guy—nothing of the troubles he had left behind at a yard sale on Maitland.

He turned left at Granby, when he saw a sign for a street sale. A year ago, he and Princeton would have come together, even though these sales were always a source of conflict between them. Princeton was always on the lookout for the rare gem, the undiscovered antique or collectible children's toy that some unsuspecting Joe was selling for a dollar, though it was worth thousands; Dylan just enjoyed the chance to look through people's junk to see what they had chosen to buy and keep for a time, then eventually get rid of, wondering at their motivation for finally parting with something they should never have owned in the first place. Princeton saw the sellers almost as enemies, dragons sitting on hoards of treasure he had to defeat with an arsenal of oration and bartering; Dylan saw them as fascinating characters whose snippets of conversation were more valuable than anything they sold. Princeton would never buy unless he saw something truly of monetary value; Dylan would buy some token at almost every sale, just to make the sellers feel better. One of their biggest fights had happened when Dylan bought a rusty old typewriter.

"It's useless!" Princeton had complained, as Dylan carried it home all the way from Isabella and Sherbourne, the iron oxide chafing reddish-brown dust onto his forearms. "What are you going to do with it?"

"Did you even talk to the guy, Princeton? This was his father's Underwood and he just wanted to feel like it had gone to a nice home. I'll put it on the balcony, with the flowerpots. It will be artistic."

"Artistic my ass." Dylan remembered the words, but couldn't quite recall the tone of Princeton's voice as he'd said it.

The first table on Granby was set up on the porch of a small duplex. A man who looked about Princeton's age was arranging objects on a card table, his chest puffed and the corners of his mouth turned in. Dylan approached him.

"How much are the wine glasses?" Sometimes the best opener was to talk about the merchandise.

"They're champagne flutes." It was a mistake that Princeton would have mocked him for, too, teased him about during the walk home, and later in bed.

"How much are the champagne flutes?"

"I'd let you have them for a quarter each."

"I'll take three, please." Dylan knew this would piss the man off—break the set, leave an odd number of glasses—it was the kind of passive aggression Dylan was really good at.

DYLAN WALKED OVER to the next table, covered with a towel and a few sad-looking items, an ashtray and a pipe and some mismatched cups and saucers. Behind the table was a lawn chair occupied by a man Dylan would put in his late seventies, staring up at him.

"Hey!" the man yelled. "I guess you're done looking through Mr. High-and-Mighty's stuff over there?"

"To be honest," Dylan said, "I wasn't too impressed. But your stuff, on the other hand..." He made a sweeping gesture and adopted a facial expression he hoped conveyed that he was suitably awestruck. And then he noticed a statuette. "What's this?"

The statuette was made of wood, and painted. It was a figurine of a man, a soldier or a sailor (Princeton would have known exactly what the figurine represented—a British guardsman or naval officer, someone from the civil war, a figure from folklore—his encyclopaedic knowledge was part of why Dylan loved him). The statuette was bent slightly forward at the hips and standing on a small platform, on top of which was a button. Dylan picked it up and pushed the button. The figure jutted forward at the hips and a ridiculously large phallus, painted in red and white stripes like a barber's pole, shot out from its crotch. The man in the lawn chair laughed so hard he had to hold his sides. "Betcha didn't see that coming!" he snorted.

"There's a lot of things I don't see coming," said Dylan softly.

"That's from 1901," the man said, still chuckling. "My mother always said when she was a girl people didn't talk about sex in public, but this sure proves different!"

"Princeton always said the same thing about his mother. That she would say she saw no reason for people to publicly acknowledge the fact they had sex at all."

"Who's Princeton, your boyfriend?"

"Husband." Dylan waggled his left ring finger at the man. "Thank you, Bill c-38."

"Good for you!" the man said. "But you're a little young to be married, aren't you?"

Dylan shrugged. Getting married had been his idea, something he'd wanted. Lots of his friends from undergrad were already married. Princeton had agreed immediately, said it was something he never thought he'd live to see. It wasn't until after the diagnosis, six months later, that Dylan began to doubt Princeton's motives.

"Well why don't you take him home this here and see if it doesn't give him a few laughs." The man reset the statuette and pressed the button, and laughed again, just as loud and hard, when the penis shot out.

"Hey, if you still get such a kick out of it, why are you selling it?"

"Well," he wiped his mouth with the back of his hand, "there comes a time in life you've got to put your toys away, I guess. I held out longer than most."

"How much do you want for it?"

"Ten dollars ought to do it."

DYLAN MADE HIS way back west, cutting up to a laneway and through the back door of his building to avoid the sale, which was probably still going on out front. He went into Princeton's bedroom. Dylan put the statue on the nightstand. Princeton's eyes fluttered open.

"Id," Princeton said, "id id ill dill idyll dilly idyll land."

"Yes," Dylan said, "it's Dylan. I'm home."

DYLAN ALWAYS THOUGHT aphasia sounded like it should be a chain of islands off the coast of the Philippines. Dylan had read his weight in articles and books on the subject, the inability to produce and/or comprehend language, and studied all the different varieties of the condition: conduction aphasia, Wernicke's aphasia, Broca's aphasia, the localizationist model vs. the cognitive neuropsychological model, nominal aphasia, and mixed aphasia, which was basically a medical term for "all of the above." Princeton's symptoms changed over time, and different doctors had differing theories about what was happening, how the condition was progressing. But no one could make any kind of improvement or promise. Princeton's brain was being damaged from the inside, by tumours the doctors compared to golf balls then oranges then grapefruits. Dylan often wondered what the next step up would be after grapefruits—cantaloupes? Watermelons? The point was, Princeton didn't have long left.

Dylan picked up the statuette and held it where Princeton could see it. He pressed the button and the man dutifully protruded out of his pants. Dylan looked at Princeton's eyes, and there was still a light on in there, he thought it was funny, and he let out strained awkward guffaws that sounded forced.

"I thought you'd like that one." Dylan reset the statue and put it back on the table. Just then one of the friends popped his head into the door—Lesley or Beverly or Evelyn—all of Princeton's friends had women's names—and gestured for Dylan to come.

"Come on, kid, we need some of those beefy twenty-seven-year-old muscles of yours. It's time to pack up for the day."

THAT NIGHT, DYLAN woke up to a strange noise. It was a chanting, a low male monotone. He got out of bed and left his room, trying to figure out where the sound was coming from. He padded down the hall in his bare feet into Princeton's room, and when he got there his heart started pounding so hard he saw spots in front of his eyes. Princeton was sitting up, eyes closed, and chanting.

"Le villi edgar manon lescaut," he said. Dylan thought it was nonsense. Neologisms—made-up words—were part of the aphasia, but Princeton hadn't been producing them for months. "La bohème tosca madama butterfly la fanciulla del west la rondine il trittico turandot."

Dylan felt the skin on his neck prickle. *La bohème, Tosca, Madama Butterfly*... He ran out into the living room, to where they had brought in the stuff that hadn't been sold. He scrambled around a bit before he found it: a collector's edition set of vinyl recordings of Puccini's operas. Not only was Princeton speaking real words, but he had listed the operas in chronological order. Dylan ran back to the bedroom.

"Benedict the sixteenth John Paul the second John Paul the first Paul the sixth," Princeton was chanting, "John the twenty-third Pius the twelfth Pius the eleventh Benedict the fifteenth." Princeton had a set of decorative plates from the Vatican, one for each pope.

"Princeton!" Dylan called, moving over to his side and shaking his shoulder, "Princeton!" Princeton opened his eyes, stopped speaking, and looked around confusedly.

"Wigwam water harpoon ha'penny hairpin pen," Princeton said.

"What happened is that you were speaking, Princeton. You were saying words." Princeton looked more confused. His receptive capabilities had been declining for weeks. "You were speaking, Princeton. You were listing Puccini's operas." Princeton looked annoyed, batted Dylan's hand away from his shoulder. He clearly didn't understand. He got frustrated quickly when that happened.

Dylan stood up, and when he did he noticed the statuette on the nightstand. It had shifted position, so that the phallus was out. "Did you touch this?" Dylan asked, "Did you push this button?" Princeton wasn't even looking at him; he had his head turned as far as it would go in the other direction. His mobility wasn't very good; it seemed unlikely he could have sat up on his own, reached over and pushed the button. Dylan wanted to reset the figurine—it seemed obscene to leave it like that for the whole night—but there was a part of him that wanted to see if anything else would happen. He told himself that the statuette had nothing to do with Princeton's strange outburst, and he thought about whether he should call one of Princeton's doctors. He decided to leave it until the morning, turned out the light, and went back to bed.

THE NEXT MORNING, which was Sunday, as he and the Lesleys or Beverlys were once again bringing things out to the sale, Dylan decided to feed Princeton himself, instead of having the home-care nurse do it. The nurse, Leshaun, always played airplane games and squealed with glee when Princeton ate something. Dylan did it more quietly, methodically, looking down at this old man's body. When they'd met, Princeton could have passed for someone in his late forties, not fifties. Now he looked far older than he was—he could be in his seventies, lying in the bed like a dead bird in the grass, light and weightless and hollow, with white stubble like lichen growing all over his face. When he was done with the feeding, Dylan had to push the statue aside a bit to set down the plate so his hands were free to wipe Princeton's mouth.

"I'm going to get rid of this statue," Dylan said. "You need to rest, and you didn't sleep very well with it beside you, did you? I'm going to put it in the sale."

Princeton didn't even try to reply.

DYLAN PUT THE statuette on the table with a ten-dollar price tag. He never tried to make money from these things. He was only selling Princeton's stuff to help with all the medical expenses OHIP wouldn't cover. And, though he hated to admit it to himself, so that he could afford a nice funeral service.

His attention wandered to an ostentatious woman who was fingering everything while talking loudly to her two girlfriends.

"Why do faggots always collect things that are *old?*" she was saying to her friends. "They're always into, like, antiques and Victorian dolls and stuff like that."

"It's because our lives are tumultuous," one of the Beverly-Lesleys said. "When your here-and-now is as fucked up as ours is, it's nice to feel like you can make some order out of the past, collect the whole set, own a little piece of history. It's making order out of chaos, baby. Now honey, why don't you and your gaggle move along. These faggots don't want to sell anything to you."

Dylan was impressed. It was a type of queeniness he'd never been good at. When he looked back at the table, the statuette was gone, a ten-dollar bill pinned to the tablecloth where it had been.

DURING THE WEEK that followed, Princeton didn't speak at all. His comprehension seemed to be getting worse as well. The doctors called this global aphasia.

Throughout the week Dylan felt a jittery agitation. He felt like he had when in foreign countries, hearing lots of language around him but no English; there were sounds and voices everywhere, but not Princeton's. Dylan longed for his voice, spent whole days trying to unearth a recording, an old video or cassette, but finding none. He tried to remember the last time Princeton had said he loved him. He thought obsessively about the dinner party where they'd met, when it was Princeton's voice, a toast he'd given, that had first aroused Dylan's interest. "To new friends," Princeton had said, looking directly at him, "and naked boys, and may they soon be one and the same." It would have sounded creepy coming from another man that age, but something about the way Princeton said it, the tone and timbre and cadence of his voice, the playful look in his eye, made it seem somehow refined, the very height of class.

SATURDAY AFTERNOON, one week after he'd bought the statuette, Dylan was shocked to see it again, this time at a garage sale up at Charles and Balmuto. It was tagged at ten dollars, just the way he'd had it.

"Where did you get this?" he asked the fat jowly woman who seemed in charge of the sale.

"A friend gave it to me the other day as a joke. It's a little too pornographic for my tastes, though—you'll never believe it—press the button at the bottom there and—"

"I know what happens," Dylan said.

HE BROUGHT IT home and placed it on Princeton's nightstand, where it had been before. He pressed the button so that the man's head jerked back and his hips shot forward and his barber-pole erection came out. Princeton was sleeping. Dylan sat on the edge of the bed, on the far side, and leaned over to whisper in Princeton's ear.

"You listen to me, Princeton. I don't care about operas or plates or any of the other stuff we're selling out there. When you get right down to it, it's the same as the crap I always bought—it's all junk. You're dying, Princeton, you know that. And what I want to know before you go is, did you know about this? Did you know, before we got married, that you were going to get sick and die, soon? Did you know I would have to take care of you, that I'd be a widower before thirty? Is that why you married me? Did you ever really love me, or did you just need a nurse to take care of you?"

But Princeton didn't answer, didn't so much as open his mouth; he simply slept.

THAT NIGHT, DYLAN couldn't fall asleep. He was on edge, listening. The trees rustling outside, the passing sirens, laughter from the street, the clocks ticking—all of it kept him awake because he was straining his ears, waiting to see if Princeton would chant again. And a little after three AM he did.

"Donna." Dylan heard Princeton moan this name, and he got up and padded towards his room. What was Donna, an opera? A play? "Frederick." Dylan stopped in his tracks. Donna was Princeton's wife, a brief marriage he'd had in the late sixties. Frederick was his son, who died of a burst appendix when he was at college. Dylan surged forward to the door, but it was stuck. It only locked from the inside, and it was impossible for Princeton to have got up and done it. He shook it, frantically, trying to get in.

"Stephen," Princeton moaned. That had been his first male lover. "Adam. Alex. Joshua." These were names Dylan didn't recognize. But he knew now: Princeton was listing the people he'd loved. "Gavin. Luke. Mason." Dylan caught his breath—Mason had been the last boyfriend before him.

"Dylan," Princeton said. "Dylan!" He called out his name so loudly, Dylan had to cover his ears.

¡FAUST

My dearest, most beloved Candace—
Today, for the first time ever, I had the thought that maybe it's better that you're gone, that you left me alone in this house for the little time I have left before I come to join you. I still miss you like the dickens, Candace, but the trouble that came home and found us today—well, I can almost say I'm glad you didn't live to see it.

It's Bartholomew. I haven't seen that layabout grandson of ours or even heard from him since the day we buried you, and today without a word of warning he just walked into the yard. I was kneeling in the garden, planting beans to see if they'll sprout in that northeastern plot where nothing ever seems to thrive except weeds. I looked up, and there he was. And he wasn't alone, either. He had this wisp of a thing with him, looked like a summer breeze would blow her over, blond and quiet and skin as pale as fresh-churned butter. I could tell from the look on their faces that they weren't here with good news.

You always said we were the closest thing that boy's had to a home, and when he left here you told him he'd always be welcome. I wasn't about to start dishonouring your wishes now. So I got up, wiped my hands on my jeans, and brought them into the house. I put out some cold cuts, mustard, and bread, even gave the boy a cold beer. I offered one to his friend, too—I'll be damned if I can remember her name—but she declined. So I figured she was in a predicament—these young girls are so strict about drinking now—and that she'd want to stay here for a while. I went to make up the guest-room, but Bartholomew stopped me. Just like that. The gall of that kid: "For God's sakes, Grandpa, I'm twenty-six years old. We'll both stay in my room." I was all set to get into it with him, in my house I run things my way, tell him that bed-sharing was what had got him into this trouble in the first place—but believe me, Candace, I just don't have the heart for it anymore. I'm an old man—I could feel my blood pressure rising, and I wasn't going to have a heart attack over it. So I kept my mouth shut.

† † †

AFTER I WROTE to you and had a bit of a nap, I spent the rest of the day in the garden, figuring those two kids needed to talk things over. I left some potatoes and carrots on the counter. I didn't say anything, but I was hoping they'd have them peeled and cut up by the time I came in. They hadn't lifted a finger: not Bartholomew, for all our trying to bring him up right, and not his mousy little friend, either. Turns out her name is Emmanuelle—French Catholic. The two of them sat there like lumps expecting me to cook for them, a prince and his princess.

Dinner was bad, Candace. Bartholomew helped himself to wine from the cellar, and he drank too much. Emmanu-elle kept asking him to stop—she calls him "Bart" on top of everything else—but he didn't listen to her. It's like he barely sees her. I think he's lost his senses. He was raving. He told me that he sold his soul to the devil.

Of all the crazy things! I've seen a lot of drunken men make bad excuses in my time, but never have I heard such utter and complete nonsense. And he really believes it. He says it's some kind of computer program that's popular now. Says he sold his soul to the devil in exchange for a career in music.

You know how he was always talking about being a rock star? Well I guess he did it. After he left here he started up a band (he called it "Dead White Doves," can you imagine?), and they got really popular. He plays guitar, and he's been all over the world performing concerts. He won two Junos, something called an "MTV Award," and then he won a Grammy. All in the past three years. Least he could have done was let me know, that's what I think. And I said so, too.

But the kid thinks all this happened because he sold his soul to the devil, and the girl seems to at least go along with it. Bartholomew says that all the famous rock stars die by the time they're twenty-seven, going out in a blaze of glory. And that's what he wanted—to be a famous rock star until he was twenty-seven, to never lose his edge or grow old. His twenty-seventh birthday is this Thursday night, and the devil's supposed to come the night before to end his life and take his soul. That's why he's here. The kid's scared out of his mind.

It's got to be drugs. He seemed so much like his mother during her really bad times... it broke my heart. Eventually I just came up to bed, left him ranting downstairs. I didn't know what else to do.

CANDACE, things are getting stranger.

Bartholomew went out today—he said he wanted to see some childhood friends in town before "the end." Emmanuelle stayed behind, and she explained things to me.

Remember when Bartholomew taught us how to use the email? And how one of us would always forget and pick up the phone while the other one was trying to send something? Well, computers have changed a lot since then. I can't believe how fast they change. Emmanuelle got the inter-web right there on our kitchen table—it's something called "wireless" that's just floating in the air all the time. Like radio waves, I guess. And she showed me this thing that Bartholomew has been yelling about, called an iFaust. It's a little star, or a pentagram, I guess, and you just plug it into the side of your computer, the same place we put the cord for the digital camera. It reeks of sulphur, this gadget, I could smell it right away. It *feels* evil, Candace, even just to look at it.

So when you put this doodad in your computer, it brings up all these things called menus, but not like any menu you or I ever saw at Mel's Diner. These "menus" list different demons, with pictures and names and symbols, hideous blasphemous things, runes and letters of the Greek alphabet and inverted Christian symbols, and you can choose to summon them or to communicate with them by the email. There's all these different choices for what you can get in exchange for your soul, promises of money and fame and talent. You can make yourself smarter or better looking, even. And there's all kinds of sexual stuff, Candace, things I didn't even talk about with the guys when I was in the army, and this girl showed it to me without even blushing.

She showed me everything. There's something called a "contract wizard" that sets up your contract for you; what you want to get in exchange for your soul, each of the different clauses and the fine print. All you have to do is click on "I Agree." I thought it was just fantasy, a pretty sick game, but she says it's real. The things computers can do nowadays— how am I supposed to tell what's real and what's not?

And she showed me Bartholomew's contract. She looked so scared and helpless. I asked her what Bartholomew had said about her predicament, if he'd offered to marry her, and she smiled and said he doesn't know yet. He's been so pre-occupied he hasn't noticed anything, and she doesn't want to worry him. Can you imagine? *She* doesn't want to worry *him*. She asked me not to tell him, and what could I say? I told her I would respect her wishes.

Every day, Candace, there are things I wish I could tell you. How I mixed sand into the varnish and covered the stairs you always thought were too slippery. The colour of paint Mrs. Peters helped me pick for the garage door this year. How terrible the choir sounds at church without you to lead it. I never wanted to be telling you anything as terrible and disappointing as what Bartholomew's done. Nothing like this.

† † †

WHEN BARTHOLOMEW GOT home, I gave it to him, my heart be damned. *How could you do this? Sell your soul to the bloody devil?* I kept screaming, as though it would change something. *We brought you up better than that!* I even brought you into it, Candace, saying that you'd be roll-ing in your grave if you knew what he'd done.

He said at first he thought it was a hoax. But when every-body started buying these iFausts, when he saw his friends actually having all their wishes come true, getting rich and famous, or suddenly developing talents they never had before, getting women and cars or whatever it was they wanted, he bought one, too—just walked into a store and bought one, for not much more than we paid for our last television. And you know what he said next? *That he thought he could trick it.* Isn't that just like him? Always trying to weasel his way out of anything resembling responsibility. He said in a lot of the folklore, people outwit the devil on some minor point, some question of interpretation. Do you know what his brilliant plan was? To set the clock on his computer back, so that it would never reach the date of his twenty-seventh birthday. But it turns out he can't do that—the computer updates automatically by satellite, something like that.

The boy is scared, Candace, that's for sure. Mad as I was, I could see that. He really thinks he's going to die the day after tomorrow. That look in his eyes. I feel sorry for him. Or I did, until he hit me with this:

Grandpa, he says, *there is another way.* Then he looks at me with those big, wet, frightened eyes, pupils as big as doughnut holes, and he says: *I'm allowed to do a trade. It's in the contract's fine print that I can trade another soul for my own.* I asked him where he thought he was going find the sorry fool to make that trade, and he looked me square in the face and said, *Well, Grandpa, the thing is—it has to be a blood relative.* Candace, I thought I was going to die right there from the shock. That kid has never given anything back to us, never a thank you, not one red cent from all of the rock star money he's apparently made, not so much as sent me a Christmas card since you died. And then he shows up with this crazy mess he got himself into, and he wants my soul to get him out of it?

He says: *You know, since you're so old, and you're probably going to die soon anyway.* Well, I lost it at that. It was everything I could do not to throw him out of the house. Sitting on my couch, and asking me to trade my soul for his? I walked right out of there. I couldn't even start writing to you for half an hour, my hand was shaking so bad.

I'm at a loss, Candace. What should I do? How do I help him? I'm going to go talk to Father Dominick tomorrow.

† † †

FATHER DOMINICK says it's real.

The Church won't say anything officially yet, but that's all internal bullshit (sorry, honey)—it's afraid to speak out against the big company that makes the iFaust. But they've been advised that the demons are real and that people's souls really are in jeopardy. If someone confesses that they've sold their soul, parish priests are supposed to offer absolution, but apparently even that doesn't always work: there's a clause in some of the contracts that says the agreement is final and negates any future sacraments or states of grace.

I asked Father Dom about the trade. He said he couldn't advise me, that he just doesn't know what the theology is. He said the trade would be a noble and charitable action—that the Church has a long tradition of rewarding self-sacrifice—but that he couldn't say for sure where my soul would end up.

What do you think I should do, Candace? I could be wrong, but I feel sure that you would take the trade. He's just a dumb kid, twenty-six years old—how can I stand by and watch him die? But I don't know that I'm ready to take his place, either.

Then there's the matter of us, honey-bear. I can't know for certain where God in His wisdom has put you, but how could you not be in Heaven, basking in His glory? If I take this trade... well, that's not where I'll be going, is it? How can I live forever without you?

Candace, what should I do?

† † †

I CAN'T DO IT, Candace. I just can't. I'm seventy-four years old, and I've spent my life making sacrifices and enduring hardships, always trying to do what I thought was right *because* it was right. Not for reward, not for fame, not even from fear of damnation, but because they were the right things to do. I'm not willing to give up the hard moral work of a lifetime to get punished for the sins of my twenty-six-year-old grandson, who gave away his most precious possession—his soul—for some record deals and a world tour.

I had made up my mind about this already, but before I went to tell Bartholomew I got Emmanuelle to show me his contract again. I read the fine print, Candace, all of it. And the anti-repentance clause isn't in there. He can repent! If he just goes to confession, says that he's sorry, he can get out of the whole thing!

But the damn fool won't do it. You know what he told me? *That he didn't believe in organized religion.* I had nothing to say to that; it was Emmanuelle who stated the obvious: *If you don't believe in it, why don't you just repent anyway?* He looked at her like she was the village idiot. He said he's not going to go kneel beside a priest inside a church and tell a lie. He says he's not remotely sorry for doing it, that it was bloody well *worth* it (though he said something much worse than "bloody"). That the only thing he regrets is not making a better deal and not including a renegotiation clause.

He's so bloody stubborn, Candace. More than you were, more than his mother was. I don't know how to react to it, how to cut through. It's nice to think the boy has a backbone and a conscience in there somewhere, but why did he choose to use it now? The whole thing makes me so damn angry I don't care what happens to him.

Of course I care. But I don't know how to show him, or what to do. I'm too old for this.

† † †

BARTHOLOMEW AND I aren't speaking to each other. There's nothing left to say. He won't repent, and I'm not willing to make the trade. We're all just sitting around the house in silence. Bartholomew is smoking. The devil is supposed to come at midnight. Two hours from now.

† † †

I HAVEN'T HEARD anything from downstairs. I'm frightened, Candace—my ticker is working overtime. Is it possible a devil made flesh is going to walk into this house—this house we lived in together for all those years—to take away our grandkid? To take his soul to Hell for all eternity?

It's too much to bear. I can't let it happen.

Forgive me, Candace, but I have to make the trade. I hope you understand. I hope that somehow our souls will be together, but if we're separated for eternity, know that I only did it to save Bartholomew. I will miss you as long as I exist. No torment of the devil can be worse than being without you. I love you forever.

† † †

OH, CANDACE—what else will I live to see?

I went down there at quarter to twelve, and as soon as I left the bedroom I could smell the sulphur. Walking down those stairs was the hardest thing I've ever had to do. *Is it here already?* I asked, but no one was in the sitting room. I found Bartholomew at the dining room table, distracted, drinking a bottle of wine and chain smoking. I wanted to tell them both about my decision right away, as I didn't think I could bear to say it more than once.

There wasn't much time left. *Where's Emmanuelle?* Bartholomew pointed at the kitchen: *She's been in there for a while.* She'd shut the French doors—first time I've seen them closed in half a decade. I could see her through the glass, standing at the counter in front of the computer. She had the iFaust plugged in, making that stink I'd thought was a devil on our doorstep. When I was about to ask what the hell she was doing, she shut the computer and looked up. She held my gaze for a second, then opened the doors and went to the table to join Bartholomew.

I took care of it, she said. *Babe, what the hell did you do?* Bartholomew said. She looked at the floor. *I had something he wanted, so I made a deal. You get to live, keep your soul. For eighteen years, the devil is going to take really good care of something that's mine, going to make it so that no physical harm can come to it, nothing bad will happen, only the good things in life. And then, it'll be his. Please don't ask me what it is—if I tell you the whole deal is off.*

Bartholomew sat there. *Pour me a glass of wine,* she said. And I knew what she'd done.

Candace, I feel so terribly, terribly old. I wish you were here. No, I don't—I wish I were with you, wherever you are. I'm done.

Angels and ministers of grace protect us.

GUTTED

The moon was full. My father laid his heavy hand on my shoulder and coaxed me awake. "Put on some shoes, boy. There's something out in the shack you need to see."

My heart buffeted my chest as I crept down the hall, past my mother's bedroom. My father would be furious if I woke her, but I wanted her to sense us, for some small creak or groan to wake her. Yet she remained softly snoring as I slipped into rubber boots, pulled a jacket over my pyjamas, and followed him into the October night.

I trudged behind him down the pathway that led from the house to his shack on the beach, the waves of the Atlantic roughly rushing up against the shore. As we got closer my boots squelched ankle-deep in thick red mud. The shack loomed, lit from inside by a flickering oil lamp, the warm glow of the flame-light seeping through the cracks in the weather-beaten wood.

We passed by my father's failed projects: the foundation he'd laid for an observatory, the rusting skeleton of a rocket ship he'd tried to construct. My father's skills were ordinary—fishing, sailing, fixing things up—but he was always trying to create the thing that would get him into the history books, show everybody that James Merrigan was more than they thought he was.

My eyes went first to the lamp—the bright purity of flame—then took in the rest of the shack: tangled nets, fishing lines of every size, hooks and knives and hatchets and saws, a dolly for loading ice blocks on and off the boat, canisters of paint, and gallons of gasoline in red plastic containers. As he slipped the little hook into the eye on the frame of the doorway, my left knee began to tremble. I grabbed my thigh with my hands to stop it; it was dangerous to show any sign of weakness.

I'D BEEN EIGHT years old when he'd shaken me and hauled me out there the last time. After weeks away at sea, he hadn't even said hello.

When we got inside he'd sat me on an upturned crate and plunked himself onto a stool, between us a bucket of fish. He'd handed me a knife the length of my forearm. "You're my son, boy," he'd said. "It's time you knew how to gut a fish."

And so, slurring and angry, he tried to teach me the things he knew. He would hold each fish firmly in his left hand, then with his right stick the knife in near the tail and run it up under the gills. With one swift motion he'd slop out the guts and cast them to a wet, bloody heap on the floor. That was the extent of the lesson, expecting me to learn just from watching.

I reached into that bucket where the fish were still thrashing, and held one belly up, vulnerable. Its scales were hard and scored small welts into my hand. Everything was too big for me, and I couldn't do it the way he wanted. I tried over and over, but I'd put the knife in too deep, or too shallow, or I'd miss the fish completely. After a couple of hours without improvement he yelled at me and cursed, "You useless piece of shit!" I was near hysterical trying to please him, and he'd grabbed the knife from my hand.

The angle was bad and the blade sliced out of the fish and through the bone of my pinky. The tip of my finger—tiny pink nail, unique little fingerprint—landed with a pathetic plop. My father just swept the fingertip into the slop pile, poured his whisky over the bleeding end, then ripped off part of his shirt and wrapped it around the stump. "You clean one fish proper. Then I'll get you all sewed up."

It took three more tries before he was satisfied.

Mother had noticed I was hiding my hand at breakfast, and when I showed it to her and told her what had happened she drove me to the hospital still wearing her nightie. As the doctor took out the messy, irregular stitches my father had made with fishing wire, she said, "You're lucky not to be infected, you know. It's a shame: if you'd brought in the fingertip right away, on ice, we probably could have reattached it."

Father stopped drinking for a week.

THE NIGHT OF the full moon, he'd barely locked the door behind him when he was across the shack, heaving something large and bulky wrapped in garbage bags. I thought it was a deer or a young moose he'd hit with his truck. I thought he'd teach me how to skin it, how to stuff and mount antlers now that I was almost a man. I had it so wrong; I should have known it would be something from the sea.

A large tail had ripped through the bottom of the bag. I was trying to recognize the fish, because I knew he would

Gutted

ask and expect me to know. Was it a tuna, a shark? Then he ripped off the plastic and turned to me with a manic grin.

"Picked her up about fifty miles out," he said. "I knew she was gold the second I saw her." I clenched up to stop my bowels from loosening. "Those assholes at *National Geographic* are gonna have to put me on the cover now."

She lay on the ice blocks he'd hauled from his boat, hard and glinting in the flickering light. I told myself I could handle this if I took it in just a little at a time. First the tail fins I'd seen peeking out from the bag, strong and wide. Then the lower body, slate grey and smooth. Halfway up was a narrow frill around her middle, and then the change from the thick skin of sea creatures to that of a human being, a belly button, well-defined abdominal muscles, then the first breasts I'd ever seen, full and round with pale green-brown nipples. I looked away, blushing, then back at the shoulders and neck, her finely featured face, peaceful, reposed, as though sleeping. I reached out. Her hands reminded me of my mother's, strong and capable, except the fingernails were shimmering like the inside of mussel shells. When I touched her finger it twitched and I jumped back with a yelp.

"Just leftover energy in the nerves," my father said, "any dead animal will do that at first. Thought I was rescuing a drowning woman until I saw that tail on her. One knock with the club was all it took."

"Who is she?" I asked, my voice small and reverential. My father misheard me.

"She's ours, son. She's all ours." And then he added, "Don't you dare tell your mother."

TELL MY MOTHER? I wouldn't have known how to start. How to tell her that Father had taken me out to his shack for the first time in five years, laid a mermaid before me, and spent half the night washing her and getting her "prepared"? How to explain the weight of that hair, the colour and texture of seaweed, bulbous and almost squeaking as I ran cold seawater over it from a bucket? How could I tell her about the ocean-grey of her eyes, which father prised open with his rough fingers, and which seemed to look at me, pleading for us to stop? How could I tell her about those breasts, my heart's flutter as I passed my hand over them, the skin cool and slightly mottled like the outside of an egg?

At breakfast my mother showed no surprise that my father was home; she simply put out three plates instead of two. When he'd shovelled in his oatmeal and gulped back his black coffee and said "I'm taking the boy out to the shack with me to work," Mother nodded, and never inquired what it was we might be working on.

OUR WORK WAS butchery.

"We're gonna see what makes her tick," he said. My father knew nothing of dissection but told me he could teach me "more than those pencil necks at school." He put on rubber gloves that went halfway up his arm and told me to hand him his knife. I wrapped my fingers around the cold rubber handle and gave it over to him, trying hard to steady my hand. He told me he was going to start with a Y-incision, like a real autopsy. It was just something he'd seen on TV when our dish was working. I stopped listening as he rambled on about the clavicle and the sternum, but I couldn't look away when he put in the blade, couldn't turn my eyes from the red grinning gash that followed the knife down the length of her body.

Gutted

Over the week he made haphazard incisions all over, cutting sideways across her one minute, lengthwise the next. The knife moved with his curiosity, no other purpose.

What drove me back each morning, other than fear of my father's wrath if I refused, was my desire to be in her presence. She was different from anything I'd ever imagined. Her smooth skin was like a dolphin's or a porpoise's. When Father cut into her, her flesh was not striated and partitioned like that of a fish, but uniformly red and bloody, like the whale meat I'd seen at the market, thick steaks laid out in rows. Whenever possible I stayed away from where he was slicing. I took to holding her hand while he "operated" on her, talking to her inside my head, telling her that it would be all right. I even named her Sydney, because Sydney was the farthest I'd ever been from home, and I imagined she came from the waters beyond that city, somewhere open and blue and far from people like my father.

AND I STARTED dreaming about her. Dreams in which the mermaid and I frolicked first in the shallows and then deep, deep under the waters of Chignecto Bay, pressed our bodies against each other in the silence of the ocean, dreams in which I kissed her cool breasts, growing ever warmer myself, until everything was heat, fire and motion and friction and waves, until in a crash I would wake up and find the very ocean had leaked out of me: salty, sharp-smelling froth that was sticky to my fingers and glimmered in the moonlight.

But the mutilations my father inflicted on her were also in my dreams. The horror was the inextricable mixture—the gaping terror of the jagged gashes, the side of her head my father had shaved of hair, the gleaming shimmer of bone where it showed—all this revulsion, and yet my body still responding and excited, whipped up like the ocean in a storm.

I HATED SEEING inside of her, the half-digested contents of her stomach—fish and seaweed and molluscs—the pale jellyfish tubes that connected her organs, the places he'd peeled back the skin and pinned it open like a lepidopterist would a butterfly. He said he wanted to figure out how she "worked" before the scientists took her, but he didn't even keep notes. The worst was when he sawed off the tail. Her spine extended all the way down to that hard, filigreed fin. It crunched when the hacksaw went through it, then thudded to the floor. I had goosebumps, was trying not to cry, the circle of backbone inside the crimson flesh like an open eye. "Tomorrow's the big day, son," my father said, wiping his brow. "They're going to send someone out from the university to take a look at what we got here. So make sure you clean up good before you come down here tomorrow. If you behave, I might let you be in the picture with me."

THAT NIGHT, I couldn't sleep. When I closed my eyes I saw her, torn apart and silent. The men in white lab coats would laugh at my father and the mess he'd made, take the mermaid away from here, subject her body to even worse things than my father's hand: cut her into many more pieces, stare at her under microscopes, and fill their vials with her blood.

I slipped out of bed. I opened my bedroom door, careful for it not to make a sound, and padded down the hallway. As I put on my boots, I felt a hand on my shoulder—my mother's. I looked at her, standing there, eyes begging to know what was going on. There was nothing I could say. I put my hand on hers, then gently pushed it off my shoulder and went out into the night.

I ran to the shack and set about my work. My pulse throbbed in the knobby scar at the end of my finger. When I was ready, I took one last look around the shack and at what

Gutted

my father and I had left of Sydney. Only her face was still intact, slender nose, pointed chin. I leaned down and kissed her cold lips.

THE MOON SAT low in the sky, waning. The waves beat against the beach the same way they always did. Traces of gasoline shone iridescent in the tidal pools, rainbow oil slicks in miniature. The wood planks crackled and popped. I heard the slap of the front door as my father ran out of the house too late, screaming, raging against what I'd done. My mother was close behind him, her long hair unfurling into the wind, trying to stop him from reaching me. They sounded distant and small as I knelt there under the stars, bathed in the heat and the smoke, awash in the orange glow, heavy flakes of ash floating down to dissolve in the ever-shifting surface of the sea.

FORGETTING HELEN

First off, beloved reader: greetings, felicitous heartfelt greetings, and welcome, and well-wishes, and an iteration of my sincere hope that you enjoy my little story. This is my first attempt at belles lettres, despite having grown up around—no, been virtually raised by—the books of the Reference Library in which I lived.

And now, dear reader—or not *now* so much as *already*—I face my first dilemma. For if I start my story at the point at which I actually begin to remember things—my divided sense of self: one half spermatozoon honed with every ion of will to the swimming, flexing my flagellum and arming my tip for the acrosome reaction; the other half ovum, waiting, spheroid, building the firmaments against any invader not myself—well, then a reader might assume I am making a political statement about Life, that life begins even *before* conception. I don't have convictions on the subject, reader, only my memories and a desire to tell you about the glorious object of my love and how the advent of desire altered me forever, which necessitates first a little about who I am, and thus my genesis.

And so, for the purpose of avoiding the appearance of grand implication-laden statements, and with a wink at Dickens and his David Copperfield (one of the greatest narrators literature has produced), permit me to start my story at the more generally acceptable, almost conventional beginning: the moment of my birth.

I WAS BORN in the library, where my parents read from opening until closing every day, where they met, where I assume they first coupled. Distracted by the birth canal and the ministrations of birthing, I cannot recall exactly which section of the library my mother was in when this event occurred, and I have never asked her. Was she among the fiction, sitting on a footstool, reading happily, releasing the maternal floodgates haphazardly in front of the regular patrons? It seems unlikely. Did she duck into the newly inaugurated Douglas Eaton Collection of Canadiana, to birth her child among the cultural artefacts of his country? Certainly not, for although the special reading room would have accorded her some privacy the risk of splashing the original diaries of Susanna Moodie would have been far too severe. It seems much more probable to me that with her predilection for instinct and perfect timing, my mother sensed the moment's approach, re-shelved her book without forgetting her place, and found an out-of-the-way corner on a quiet floor before experiencing even the first contraction of her labour. It would not surprise me if my father was oblivious to the entire thing, lost in a book; nor if he knew what was happening and headed off to find a volume on midwifery, only to miss the actual event; nor again if he knelt there beside her, holding my mother's hand, gently and silently encouraging her. One thing is certain: my mother, always conscientious, polite, and rule-abiding, did not scream. My mother has never spoken to me above a whisper, and there is no way she would have changed this behaviour no matter what the pain. I imagine she lay down on those somewhat dirty carpets—colour-coded by floor, smelling of illicit coffees and dust motes and the soles of shoes—and sweated and panted and pushed without ever crying out. My mother's son, I too remained silent as I slid into the world. My mother wrapped me in a blanket and I fell asleep, allowing her to deliver the afterbirth, and, after regaining her composure, to carefully dispose of it in the ladies' washroom.

The story of my afterbirth, if you'll allow the tangent, does not end there at all: I know because I am familiar with the woman who discovered it, a certain María Fuentes, matron of the custodial staff at the reference library. While she hadn't met my parents previous to my birth (the library being very large), she soon became something of a nurse-maid to me, a nanny and babysitter and grandmother in one solid and sturdy form. She often told me of her shock that day when, rifling through the trash in the third-floor women's washroom, she found a blood-stained paper towel wrapped around a pulpy mass. (Her searching through the garbage creates rather a desperate image, but it had nothing to do with compulsion—she was simply doing her job: you see, as the library houses many rare and important and therefore valuable books, and as all of the books are non-circulating, there is a certain tendency for less respectful patrons to deface them or attempt to steal from the holdings. One ingenious thief (or series of thieves—as no one was ever caught we can't be sure whether this particular manner of heist was conceived of by one person who performed it many times, or one person who disseminated the method to many,

or many people who came up with the same idea at approximately the same time, as seems to happen with human
beings and their inventions, as with the helicopter and the
light bulb and the telephone) took to throwing books out—
simply placing them in the trash—and then rooting through
the beat-up dumpster in the alley outside under the cover of
night and walking away with whichever books s/he wished.
I say ingenious because it involved not only realizing that
the garbage is taken out through a staff-only service door
that was not equipped with sensors (the designers assuming,
somewhat fallaciously, that no staff would ever attempt to
steal a book), but also a fair amount of planning and dedication. In any case, once the library discovered that this was
happening (due in part to a week in which clear garbage bags
were used instead of black ones), but before they could pay
for and install sensors on the staff doors, they asked Maria
Fuentes to check the garbage receptacles for books as she
emptied them. Maria Fuentes scowled when she was asked,
to show that she was not thrilled at the prospect of sifting
through garbage, but in actuality she loves the library and
its books and she deplores thieves and was excited that she
could have some role in stopping them. So excited, in fact,
that she continued searching through the garbage even after
the sensors were installed, and continues to do so *to this
day*, on the premise that plucky thieves might cut the sensor
strip out of the book before throwing it out, thus beating the
system.) She was more concerned than curious, and more
curious than disgusted, when she found the bloody paper
towel, and as she is a woman of considerable experience she
recognized what it was at once. After her mild shock sub-
sided, and being somewhat superstitious, Maria Fuentes
decided to keep the afterbirth she had found, to cure it and

dry it and grind it into a powder. Later, after meeting my parents (and me), and becoming our closest family friend, she still refused to tell me why she did this, and would only say that the pulverized afterbirth was very powerful and that she would give it to me when I was old enough and the time was right. I couldn't imagine what power it could possibly hold, but I had come to trust the ways of Maria Fuentes and had long since stopped asking her questions that I knew she would not answer (for instance, how old she was or exactly where she came from or why the rest of the custodial staff regarded her with such an air of fearful wonder).

I slept for the majority of the first day of my life, and on the second day my mother began teaching me to read. She accomplished this by writing a word above each of her nipples with a blue ballpoint pen, and, in the early days, drawing the corresponding image beside the word. As I fed, she would direct my eyes to the contours of the letters, whisper the word to me with perfect enunciation, and emphasize the sounds of the diphthongs and combinations of consonants, the labials and bilabials and fricatives and liquids and palatals and dentals, the way these work together to make units of sound and meaning, and how we represent them in written form. I would break the sucking seal and say the word with my toothless gums and tiny pink tongue and my mother would smile and only then would I allow myself to fall asleep. But by the time I was two, and my mother had written SESQUI- above one nipple and PEDALIAN over the other, we knew it was time to for me to be weaned and read on my own, to read from the infinite pages in the stacks around me. She had given me a love of reading and a penchant for tattoos.

Forgetting Helen

ALTHOUGH HE SPOKE to me more loudly than my mother, perpetually darting his eyes over the frames of his reading glasses to scan for librarians and patrons, my father was an essentially quiet man with an unassailable equanimity. His contribution to my upbringing most often came in the form of providing me with insight into, or helping me to analyze, some obscure text or ideology that was troubling me. He was a doting mentor, suggesting books for me to read and discussing them with me afterwards, delighting in my delights and thoughtfully considering my criticisms and questions, exorcising ambiguity and ignorance with an indefatigable patience. I loved him differently than I loved my mother, but as completely and overwhelmingly.

One morning when I had just turned four, we were discussing *Crime and Punishment*, specifically the (im)morality of the protagonist in killing an unscrupulous pawnbroker. We had brought an English translation of the book down to the cool ground floor, and were seated cross-legged in a far corner, undisturbed. A spider crawled forth through some subterranean fissure in the library's architecture and began to glide across the white carpet in front of us.

I had read about them, of course. The itsy-bitsy spiders of nursery rhyme and song, the spider who sat beside Miss Muffet as she ate her curds and whey, the various tales of the trickster Anansi or Kwaku Ananse from our African folklore section, the beneficent and brilliant Charlotte spinning her web to save the hapless pig Wilbur, the giant Aragog in the Harry Potter series, Tolkien's giant spiders of Mirkwood and the evil Shelob in her layer in the Ephel Dúath mountains, the small black spider Paul Farenbacher coaxed from inside a young girl's ear in Sarah Selecky's short story, Arachne of Dante's *Purgatorio*, and whole textbooks filled with descriptions of the forty thousand different species of spiders, the Black Widow and the Trapdoor Spider, the Portia Spider and the Goliath Birdeater, the Wolf Spider and the Sydney Funnel-web—but never, ever had I seen one.

I watched it, mesmerized and frozen, as it came towards us. Then it crawled onto the back of my hand, tickling me with a feathery sensation that sent tingles prickling all the way up my arm, giving me goosebumps. I screamed—a short, scared cry—and drew my hand back on instinct. The spider fell, righted itself, and began to scuttle away at a slightly more rapid pace. I raised a fist and moved to strike, like Raskolnikov with his axe, and in another second I would have transmuted that spider from a living creature to a smear on the carpet. But my father restrained my arm, swept me up and moved me back two feet, then plucked an envelope from his breast pocket and held it open in the spider's path until it crawled inside. Then he closed the envelope and handed it to Maria Fuentes, who had appeared from wherever she'd been a mere instant after my scream.

"Please take this poor little fellow outside, Maria," my father said. "He's not where he belongs." Then he turned to me with a serious expression.

"You have read about spiders, son. Other women and men have looked at spiders, observed them, bred them, kept them, interacted with them in the world, imagined what they would be like in other worlds not our own. And you can know all that they know, because they have written it down and you have read it. But that is a different type of knowledge altogether than *experience*, what it felt like to let this spider crawl over your hand, or how terrible it would have felt to have killed it. The library is for reading only, experiencing the world as distilled by the thoughts and lives of

Forgetting Helen

others, through language and story. The library is quite separate from the outside world: protected and apart. Your mother and I have chosen to live here—to know the world through reading alone. That is the life you are born to."

I nodded, for I understood, and wanted only to be as wise and gentle and learned as my parents. But that night I lay restless, agitated, able to think of nothing but the strange tickling sensation that had briefly electrified the back of my hand.

FAST FORWARD NOW to my second birth—if you'll allow the characterization—that second birth of adolescence, and presume for me the images and all those gerunds you know to be applied to the awakening of young men to their bodies' sexuality: sprouting, hardening, growing, spurting, fluttering, swelling, bursting, ripening, sweating, trembling, surging, inflating, tugging, emerging, maturing, yanking, stiffening, shooting, gushing, budding, enlarging, quivering, jerking, squirting, radiating, erupting, expanding, emitting, and lusting—above all the lusting. There are few forces in nature as powerful, insatiable, and all-consuming as a teenage boy's lust. But pheromones and hormones affect not just the body, but the psyche as well. More than the physical rigor of lust, which I could slake at my will in the lavatories or downstairs in the cool basement at night (I was never fully satisfied with this activity, though I enjoyed its ephemeral ecstasy and tried it often enough), what burned and tortured me most was my desire for companionship and mutual affection—I wanted more than anything on earth to be in love.

From the dusty translations of the oldest human texts in the back corner of the fifth floor to the shiny postmodern

American fiction on display in the bright lobby, every book I knew had something to say about love. I knew, for instance, that it was something difficult, powerful, dangerous, uplifting, transformative, worth dying for; I knew when it was true it lasted forever; I knew that men would travel to the very ends of the earth in search of it, overcome all obstacles to return to it, would even kill for it, but I knew very few specifics—let alone how to find it in my life. When I asked my father about love he would get a distant look in his eye and tell stories about my mother when she was young, how she read Russian aloud to him with a northern accent he found adorable, pronouncing all the unstressed O's, and how her fair hair hung past her knees and how he would read her versions of the Rapunzel tale whenever he could find them. When I asked my mother about love she would look worried and tousle my hair in a way she hadn't done in years. Maria Fuentes would smile and say that I'd learn about such things soon enough and in my own way. All I knew for sure was that at its core love meant the complete physical, spiritual, and emotional union of two people: a man and a woman.

And the woman I loved the most, the woman I returned to again and again in my fantasies, the woman whose essence I most wanted to find in contemporary flesh, was Helen of Troy.

Oh, she may not seem a logical choice to you, but when has there ever been logic in the realm of love?

For those of you here moved to answer me—for I doubt not that there are readers out there who think they have applied logic to love, or know some anecdotal tale about an unfortunate fool who did—"unfortunate" being a rather judgmental word, for which I ask your forgiveness, but on this point my opinions are strong and clear (or at least, they were at the time I am writing about and cannot be compromised)—for those readers, let me ask you not to interrupt my story with your answer now: I mean the question to be rhetorical.

I loved Helen. The face that launched a thousand ships, inspired a war, the daughter of a god. I imagined myself a Trojan king, lying with her in the hold of my bireme, crossing the ocean, not daring to look behind lest the sails of her husband's armada were in pursuit. I imagined all the men who wanted and desired her, how furiously all men who'd seen her would excite themselves, and how they would stare with envy and admiration at me, who claimed and satisfied her. I imagined holding her in my arms, knowing she was the most beautiful woman on earth, the zenith of all that was feminine, pressing my lips against hers. I imagined her silk dresses and chiton, the way the fabric would run between my fingers, the breathy whisper of it as it slipped off her shoulders and gathered around her ankles at the floor. I imagined our wedding, attended by the most powerful rulers in the land, all of them jealous and quietly fuming. I imagined the children we would have, reading bedtime stories to cherubic faces before retiring to pursue pleasures of our own. I imagined the poem she would read to me on our fortieth wedding anniversary, in perfect dactylic hexameter.

Who, if not Helen? She was the first woman in Western literature who moved me, the first whom I could imagine as a real person in flesh before me. Aristocratic, learned, skilled in domestic arts, regal and renegade, passionate, tragic. Her image floated up each time I closed my eyes, inspired by the verses of the ancients and the paintings of Jacques-Louis David, Evelyn de Morgan, Dante Gabriel Rossetti, Lord

Frederick Leighton, and many, many others. I contemplated what it meant to be married to a king, abducted by another, pursued by scores of Greeks who made ripples in history still being felt in modernity. Who else should I love, who else should I try to find in this life?

ON MARCH 29 of the year I was seventeen, at 1:13 PM, I saw the most beautiful hand in the history of the world, and knew at once that I had found my love, my real-life Helen. I was walking through the stacks looking for a play by Michel Tremblay, and as I reached the end of a row, a table came into my field of vision—an ordinary table, rectangular and made of varnished oak like every other in the library—but on this table I could see a length of forearm covered by a flowing blue sleeve and an incredible, delicate, exquisite hand.

A hand, you think? Just a hand? No. It gave off its own light, I swear to you. I stood transfixed, capable only of contemplating the hand. It could have been carved from marble, lying on the table in a relaxed pose. It was not splayed coarsely out nor held artificially prim; it simply rested. The fingers were long and slender, the ring finger longer than the index finger, a trait that signalled great beauty and intelligence according to the Egyptians and the Greeks. The fingers were a pianist's dream, a violinist's fantasy, a surgeon's coldest envy—I could see just by looking at them that they were agile and deft. The hand looked absolutely still and yet entirely capable of motion. Majestic metacarpals! Trapezium and scaphoid and pisiform, capitate and hamate and lunate, symphony of tendon and bone and muscle! Each digit ended in perfection, cuticle healthy, nail round and trimmed and clean, with clear polish applied tastefully. The thumb lay not so much in opposition to the fingers as in counterpoint to them, in harmony with the larger mechanism of the hand. The hand, very simply, made me tremble.

And then I was distracted. A short woman with a large handbag tapped me on the shoulder and asked me to move out of her way; she needed a book that was behind me. I complied, awkwardly shuffling aside in the cramped aisle (the library is octagonal with an opening in the centre that extends from the lobby all the way to the ceiling of the fifth floor—so the aisles, like the spokes of a wheel, have plenty of room near the exterior walls, nearly none closer to the centre railing, where I was). My view obstructed, I rushed down the length of the next aisle only to find necking college students blocking my way, navigated around them, then finally reeled back into the previous aisle where my love was sitting. But when I turned and looked for the hand I now loved, it was gone. The table and chair were empty ("empty" does such a poor job of conveying the utter lack of essence, the cosmic vacuum now surrounding that table, but "empty" is still the best word I can come up with after searching the thesaurus exhaustively for a suitable synonym). There was no bag or open book to indicate my love would be returning. I panicked. I had to find her. I started rushing around, up and down the aisles parallel, but nothing. I scanned the stairs, the press of hands in the clear glass elevator; I strained over the railing to view the entire open enclave of the lobby, but Helen was gone.

LONG, LONG, DID I pine for that hand! And how I cursed that woman and her loathsome book in the days to come! At first I was so miserable I could barely read, simply moping around the stacks, dragging my finger along the spines of the books, selecting nothing. Then I began to fantasize wildly. I could attach no body or face to the hand when conjuring it in my mind: while surely it belonged to my modern-day Helen, I could not begin to conceive of what she would look like. The hand was the only real thing I had ever lusted after, the only image that hadn't come from a book or my own imagination. I sketched the hand in charcoal and pencil and ink, drawing from memory and checking my representations against books on art and sculpture. I hoarded medical and kinesiology textbooks, any manuals on anatomy and the body that contained detailed images of hands, piling them into the study cubicles on the crimson-carpeted second floor and poring over them day and night. I looked through books about American Sign Language as though they were pornography, imagining the hand I loved contorting into the different positions pictured there, imagining it was my love's hand grasping me instead of my own. The patrons began to notice me lurking about, staring at hands, waiting to match any I found to the ideal hand, which I now knew existed, which I hoped desperately to find again.

A YEAR AND six weeks passed and it was early May, the orange light of sunset casting long rectangles through the windows onto the floor. I was half-heartedly skimming through a David Adams Richards novel and wandering the stacks. At the end of a page I happened to look up, and it was exactly as before: I could see a hand and a little bit of forearm resting on a table. I recognized it. I rushed forward.

The hand was more perfect than I remembered, exceeded all the pale copies I had imagined and made. This time, the fair skin was not contrasted against the fabric of a sleeve, but transitioned seamlessly to wrist and gorgeous forearm. The forearm was covered in the most finely detailed tattoo I had ever seen. Its script (I immediately recognized the script was from the Nordic family, and later research confirmed it to be Icelandic), wrapped around the arm, and between the lines of text were brushstrokes of colour in waves, moving through the colour spectrum like a rainbow as they ascended to the elbow. The upper arm was also tattooed, hard to make out under the sleeve of the t-shirt, but looking like an icon of some medieval saint.

But it was the face that shocked me. The face—the body—belonging to the hand I loved, was male. My Helen was a man. I stood there simply taking him in. He was about my age, slouching at the table, reading a textbook on abnormal psychology. His mouth hung slightly open as he read, and he moved a finger under the text as he went along—a habit I usually deplored but forgave because of the exquisite beauty of the finger employed. He had dark eyelashes that made it look almost as though he were wearing eye makeup—which I suppose he could have been. What I couldn't understand was that I was still excited. As much as I was shocked and disbelieving and unmoored, I was still enrapt, the hand was still beautiful. I had to touch it.

I rushed forward before I could change my mind, and slid the pads of my fingers over the warm skin of his hand and let my fingers fall between his upon the open page. It was better than anything I had read about, better than what even the most divine poetry and prose concerning love's first touch could possibly convey.

He took me by the wrist and moved my hand away from his. He dropped my arm and gently pushed me back a step, then he took his perfect hand and flexed it twice, unaware of the tremors shivering up and down my legs from seeing the hand in motion. "Look," he said, "I'm not sure what you think is going on here, but I'm really not interested. Back off." And with that he shut his book and moved away.

IT WAS A moment of epiphany and tragedy, beloved reader. I am not ashamed to say Maria Fuentes found me in the stacks, weeping, and asked me what was wrong. She wiped my tears with the same rough brown paper towel with which the library had stocked the washrooms my entire life, and listened calmly to my story. She was patient and kind. She told me I needed to discover a new point of view, and took me through one of the few doors in the library I had never opened—the one that opened onto the corridor that led to metal stairs with industrial grip-strips, leading in turn to the door to the roof. She opened this second door and stepped through, but I was too afraid to follow her—I had never left the confines of the library before. The sunlight was too bright, the wind too loud—I wasn't ready. Maria Fuentes sighed and shook her head as she shut the door, and encouraged me to find my parents and tell them what had happened.

My parents too were very gentle and seemed wholly unsurprised. My father showed me in which sections to look for stories that would help me understand the transition I was facing. With his help I scanned for authors that could tell me more about what it meant for a man to love a man— Edmund White and Christopher Isherwood, James Merrill and Sky Gilbert, Derek McCormack and R.M. Vaughn, John Barton and Billeh Nickerson, and many others. But for the first time in my life, books were not enough. None of them contained even a glimmer of what I had felt the moment I touched the hand.

Forgetting Helen

In my mind I started the business of forgetting. Forgetting all that I had read about men and women, their kind of love, forgetting the literary women I had thought would be the models against whom I could compare the real women in my life, forgetting Tess of the d'Urbervilles and Dante's Beatrice, Russell Smith's coffee-skinned urban beauties, and, more slowly, with the most difficulty, forgetting Helen.

I shifted from her to her suitors and their friends, to Paris and Priam and Achilles, Hector and Ajax and Agamemnon, what it would feel like to fist my fingers in a thick beard and pull the mouth of a man to mine. I thought less of Helen in her ship, watching the war progress distantly, and more of the rigid silence of men's bodies in the dark belly of the Trojan Horse, what it would have been like to endure that night, pressed soldier against soldier inside that roughly hewn cavern, how hot breath would have blown across my neck, how the weight of men would have pressed hard against my body, how perspiration would have dripped heavy from our glands in the thick and stifling swelter, how our hearts would thrum with anticipation for the brutal, bloody task before us.

FOR TWO YEARS I lived a dull existence in the library, increasingly dissatisfied with paper and vellum and cardboard, with musty carpet and fluorescent light, with reading about what others had imagined and experienced while only ever reading myself. Finally I fell victim to a self-indulgent listlessness that none could shake me out of.

It was without anticipation or joy that I lay down to sleep on the eve of my twenty-first birthday. It was with annoyance and a feeling of misanthropy that I awoke to the lilac-scented hands of one of the custodial staff squeezing my shoulders and neck.

"Wake up," she whispered. "There is a great surprise prepared for you."

I followed her, wiping the sleep from my eyes. She brought me to the back stairs on the fifth floor, the stairs that led up to the roof. My mother, father, and Maria Fuentes were all gathered there. I allowed them to usher me up, still afraid but now willing, onto the rough asphalt.

Light seemed to come from every direction. The sun was rising, my favourite shade of cream soda pink, glinting off the glass of the skyscrapers downtown, reflecting off the cars snaking through the streets, streaking the sky with colour. Pedestrians moved like punctuation marks on the distant sidewalk; the sounds of traffic reached my ears for the first time. Through the city ran streams of potential and motion. The air was the freshest thing I had ever breathed, and carried whiffs of what I thought to be exhaust, flowers from window boxes, hot tar in the sun. I was heady with new sensation.

"I never knew," I said. "I never knew it could be like this."

The three of them smiled as if to say they knew more than I but didn't fault me for it, and each of them gave me a gift. From my father, a map of the subway system, well-worn and taped in the corners. From my mother, a pen and a journal, inside which she had written *"Aardvark" to "zygote" you learned at my breast; of all that's been written, you've read here the best.* And Maria Fuentes was holding a small cloth bag with a powder inside.

When I opened it, it took me a moment to realize what it was. "But I don't know what it's for," I told her.

"Watch," she said. She reached into the bag for a pinch and shot her arms into the air, releasing the powder in a cloud. It swirled around me like a small cyclone; then the wind took it, dispersed the particles in all directions

Forgetting Helen

and blew them about the city. "We cannot protect you from the heartbreaks of a life lived in the world, but you will always be welcome and safe in the place you were born," Maria said. "When the library is too far from you, scatter this powder wherever you are, and the safety and comfort of this place will come to you. Now, wherever the wind blows in this city, you will be at home." I clutched the bag to my heart.

"Now go," my mother whispered. I turned from their smiling faces, terrified and excited, and went back down the metal steps to the electric blue carpet of the fifth floor, past the yellowed tomes of the ancients in dual-language editions, laid out in Greek or Latin or Hebrew on one side of the page, English on the other; over to the spiral stairs, down onto the fourth floor, with the vertical files of photographs and all the periodicals in which I loved to read the news of the world, the *Guardian* and the *Wall Street Journal* and the *Times of India* (India! Perhaps now I could go there!); down onto the third where the oversized art books stuck out akimbo from the shelves; down to the passionate red carpet of the second floor, barely glancing at the table where I had first seen the hand, smiling as I passed the cookbooks (mostly at *The Naked Chef* by Jamie Oliver, whose hand squeezing a lemon had been one of the best of the pale copies of the hand I'd sought); down onto the first floor with the white carpet and the shiny new fiction books in glossy paperback with loud neon covers, past the bronze bust of Archimedes, past all of this and past the circulation desk and through the metal detectors to the very edge of the lobby itself.

I looked back at what had always been my home. I looked up and on the top floor, leaning over the railing, I saw my parents, reading glasses hanging on chains around their necks, waving crazily but silently from above. Then I closed my eyes, took a deep breath, opened my eyes again to stare directly at the leaded glass of the library door, and walked out into the world.

THE GRIMPILS

Marsha knows why this is happening to her family. It's because of something terrible she did last September. She was looking in on her son, just wanting to see him sleeping. He was fourteen, and had just started grade nine.

She walked into his room and turned off the desk lamp, noticed his open notebook and a math textbook in which nothing looked familiar from her own years in high school.

He was sleeping on his side, facing away from her. She leaned over and brushed his hair back from his forehead, kissed him, felt his temperature out of a mother's habit of care. Her fingers touched the thin white scars that crossed his back.^M

M (Marsha footnotes wounds) Inflicted years ago by the neighbour's ferret, Fenwick, the cuts ran angry from his left shoulder to his right hip, a parade master's sash of injury. The three parallel lines of hurt made him cry, tears that had soaked Marsha's t-shirt at the shoulder. She'd cleaned the cuts, the peroxide foaming and foaming with its stinging hiss. The thin gouges pulled apart in the night, like the lashed backs she'd seen in movies, opening under white linen togas in thin red lines.

When Toby was little Marsha used to sit up at night, Alan slumbering far and heavy beside her, and imagine a super-computer calculating all the things that might harm her son. She wanted a comprehensive list so she could prevent each one from happening, longed for this printout of peril so badly that she could feel its crisp paper pressed between the pads of her fingers.

She read books about parenting, talked her husband into relocating to a safer neighbourhood, bought accident insurance, found good schools, made an effort to be available without smothering, and worked to keep her kid away from cigarettes and drugs and kidnappers. She did all the things a mother could do, but there was no way to fight it all. In the end, parenting was damage control; parenting was failure.

He was sleeping shirtless, something he'd started doing at thirteen to be more like his father. He still had a boy's frame—skinny shoulders, hairless arms—and the air in the room was getting cool, so she lifted the sheet to cover him. As she did he rolled onto his back and she saw his stiff erection sticking up at her out of his boxers. It seemed gargantuan, disproportionate on her little boy's body, and it struck her how much it looked like Alan's, her husband's, penis. She reached out to tuck him back into his shorts, a small adjustment, one of the million maternal tasks her hands performed each day, and the penis twitched, jerked up slightly with some involuntary contraction of muscle.

She lowered the sheet and left the room, quickly as she could.

Now, every time something bad happens, Marsha thinks it's because she didn't put that sheet down fast enough.

RICHARD AND LOUIS met Nick Grisholm at the Café Sans Souci.[R] They were waiting for Marsha. It was Paris, it was springtime, but Richard stared silently into his tea, resting his left hand on the warm family-sized teapot he always ordered, the second mug it came with unused beside him. Louis dumped packets of sugar into his café au lait. He didn't like coffee, but it was the only thing he knew how to order in French, and he was too embarrassed to reveal this to Richard. They both looked up at the same time as a man strode quickly across the café from the door's tinkling bell to the polished marble counter. He filled the air with a hum of buzzing worry. Many others in the café were also watching, because he was expensively dressed and had the face of a GQ cover model.

Louis and Richard read each other's eyes—they knew that air of frantic preoccupation well—this man was here to find a Grimpil. Louis made a gesture to say *No, no, you sit; I'll take this one,* and got up from the table.

"Excuse me, sir—oh? You are English, aren't you?"

"American. Leave me alone." The man—Nick—spoke loudly but through clenched teeth.

"OK, right, I'm doing this all wrong." Louis glanced over his shoulder to meet Richard's stare. He leaned in and said, more softly, "Listen, why don't you come sit down with us—"

"Why would I do that?" He talked so that everyone in the café could hear him.

R (Richard footnotes traditionally) The Café Sans Souci is located on Rue de Franqueville, not far from the Bois de Boulogne. The closest Métro stop is La Muette.

The Grimpils

"You're making a scene. And *we* know what you're going through." For a moment they looked into each other's eyes,[L] then Nick followed Louis back to the table. Richard had already pulled over another seat, so there were four including the one for Marsha.

Nick folded himself into the chair and rested his elbows on the table and his head in his hands, a compressed accordion, suddenly empty of air and noise.

"I'm Richard; you've met Louis, my partner." As he said this, Richard turned over the never-before-used mug, and poured a cup of tea.[N]

THERE WERE THOUSANDS of women like Marsha, women whose sons had gone missing; there were thousands like Nick and Louis and Richard, whose partners or loved ones had vanished. There were thousands deserted by the men and teenage boys who had tended to isolate themselves and prefer each other's company, who'd suddenly abandoned their lives.

They had left their homes in all the English-speaking countries and spilled into Paris, arriving in droves. Whole planeloads of men with fashionable haircuts and coordinated outfits, pants of leather and vinyl, Lycra and spandex, nasal voices and outlandishly elaborate gestures. They sparkled, talked to each other at inappropriate volume,

---

L (Louis footnotes colour) Nick's eyes were acid green, tiny glass apothecary bottles, sitting dusty on window ledges (letting through the light), holding something dangerous.

N (Nick footnotes scents) The tea was Ceylon, but smelled too of cinnamon and nutmeg, with just a grace note of some dark berry: blackberry, blueberry, or currant.

compared stories of where they'd come from and who their favourite celebrities were, which music they *really* liked. They were unified in their search for the Author, the one who appeared in all their dreams, who had awakened them from their slumber and brought them to the warm embrace of Paris.

"LOUIS AND I were just waiting for a friend of ours." Richard slid the milk and sugar across the table. "Marsha is in Paris looking for her son, Toby. Louis and I came here looking for Joseph, my nephew whom we're raising. And I suspect you're looking for someone too."

Nick's face turned pale.[L]

"He didn't know," Louis said, turning to Richard. This habit of Louis's to state the obvious about some person who was right there but address the comment only to him, Richard found infuriating.

"You didn't know there were others?"

Nick shook his head.

"It's alright." Richard placed his hand on Nick's forearm. "Why don't you tell us what happened?"

Nick tilted his mug towards himself and stared into it, letting out a sigh. He hadn't told anyone at home the reason for his trip—he'd only informed a few key people (his parents, his boss, his neighbour) that he was going away at all, and hadn't said to where. But there was something about these men—an openness in Richard's face, invitational and gentle despite his slightly formal air; a quiet melancholy that hung about Louis—and it felt like the right moment to let it out.

L It was a blush reversed: rosy pinks receding, leaving the colour of hard-boiled egg.

"My boyfriend of eight years, Tom, left me and flew to Paris looking for some... some writer." Richard and Louis said the writer's name in unison and Nick looked surprised again. Louis offered him a swig from the flask he kept in his pocket. Nick uncapped it, shook it slightly under his nose,[N] and took three long swallows.

He and Tom had met at the Pride Parade in San Diego, and despite not being each other's type, after years of club lineups and still being there when the lights turned on and one-night stands that left them feeling empty and used, they'd fallen headlong in love. They'd found an apartment and decorated it with Tom's kitsch—posters of Björk and Marilyn Monroe-shaped floor lamps. Nick had dragged Tom antique shopping to find the perfect footstool or end table, and they'd laughed at how stereotypical they were being, urban queers making day trips to the country. While Tom caught up on his Hollywood gossip magazines on the balcony, Nick would watch sports on TV. Their lives were, more or less, ideal.

Then things started getting weird. Tom started reading books, which Nick found a welcome improvement, leaving copies of David Leavitt and Alan Hollinghurst around the apartment, but Tom would only read books by this one writer, a gay guy who wrote funny essays about his odd jobs and his boyfriend and his family. Tom couldn't stop talking about him. Tom downloaded all the radio programs on which this writer had ever appeared, his distinctly recognizable voice one step down from Truman Capote's infamous whine, programs like *This American Life* and *Shout*

N Sweet: sugared almonds, the abrasive whiff of ethanol; the flask's metal, coppery like blood.

It Out! and *Stories for Dangerous Times*. Tom dreamt about the guy, in a very unsettling come-to-me-my-chosen-ones kind of way, and then Tom started saying that whenever he read the writer's books the smell of flowers filled the room,[N] getting stronger and stronger and urging Tom to act. One day Nick came home to find the apartment empty and a note saying Tom had left for Paris to find the Author and wait for further instructions.

When Nick finished his story there was a brief and respectful silence, interrupted by Marsha bustling into the café. A small trickle of blood congealed on her forehead.[M] She took the remaining seat—drops of perspiration had formed along her brow. Richard dabbed at her face with a cloth napkin, and signalled to the waiter for a glass of water.

"Marsha," Richard said.

"I haven't had any luck, Richard, no luck at all. I just can't believe no one's seen him. He must be here, they're all still here, aren't they? Are there less of them, do you think? They do move around, though. Every time I show his picture they just shrug, say he could be anybody."

"Marsha," Richard said again, "this is Nick. Nick's boyfriend has taken a trip to Paris without any warning. Louis, are you done with your café au lait?" Louis nodded, not

---

N The way Tom described it to Nick, it was not like smelling one flower or a bouquet of cut flowers, or entering a flower shop, or even walking nervously into a funeral home for the viewing of a very popular person, but like being in a greenhouse or a botanical garden in spring when everything is blossoming, like standing right inside the centre of a red carnation and breathing in its air.

M The scrape was caused by a low-hanging branch Marsha crashed into in the wooded section of the Bois de Boulogne; red oozed through the break in the skin, slowly and thickly dripping down.

having taken a single sip. "We should go back to the hotel.[R1] Everyone is staring at us, and we could probably all do with a little privacy."

MOST GRIMPILS HAD left their home countries in haste, without a lot of luggage or enough money for a long stay in Paris. Many of the Grimpils—and definitely, Marsha felt sure, her own fifteen-year-old son and Louis and Richard's seventeen-year-old nephew—were taking advantage of the summer weather[N] and living outdoors. The two most populated parks were the Bois de Boulogne in the west and the Bois de Vincennes in the east. Today Marsha was taking Nick with her to show him around, and heading north, to the Parc départemental de La Courneuve,[R2] a conservation area four hundred hectares in size—outside the core of the city and expansive enough to accommodate tens of thousands. As they waited for the bus, Marsha listed off the other parks where Grimpils were known to be living: Parc de la Butte du Chapeau-Rouge, Parc départemental Jean Moulin, Parc des Beaumonts, Parc de Monceau, Parc des Guilands, Parc des Buttes-Chaumont, Parc du Champs de Mars, Palais du

---

R1 Hôtel Jeanne d'Arc le Marais, at 3 Rue de Jarente, +33 (0)1 48 87 62 11, nearest Métro: Saint-Paul. Marsha's single occupancy room was sixty euros per night, Louis and Richard's eighty-four. Richard enjoyed the irony of staying in a hotel named after a woman famous for hearing and obeying voices, but he kept this delight private, fearing his friends would think him macabre or insensitive.

N Nick could smell the Seine, freshly cut grass, the last lilacs, and the scent of hot sidewalk.

R2 Richard had told Marsha that the locals unfailingly referred to the park simply as La Courneuve, but she insisted on using the park's full name as written on maps.

Chaillot, and all the civic gardens, Jardin des Plantes, Jardin du Luxembourg, Jardin des Tuileries. Nick's mind wandered as Marsha's list went on and on, the movements of her
mouth choppy and awkward around the French words.

La Courneuve encompasses several different types of ter-
rain, from woods to shrubs to meadows to fields and lakes,
to an eight-hectare lagoon. Marsha wanted to spend time in
the grassy area near the lagoon, although once they got there
she found the soft ground difficult to walk through, and was
frustrated by the fact there weren't any trees on which to
staple the posters of Toby she'd printed from the courtesy
computer in the hotel lobby. They walked through the tall
grasses towards the water. Nick reached back to help Marsha, whose shoe had come off in the sludge, and when they
continued on he squeezed her hand without meaning to.

There were men of all ages sunbathing and playing in
the water, many of them naked—wrestling, swimming,
embracing, scrubbing themselves with face cloths stolen
from hotels, lathering shampoo into their hair, lazing in the
shallows. The sun glinted off their wet torsos; the brightness
of all that flesh made Nick squint.

"Oi!" a snarky British voice came out of nowhere, "a couple of breeders come down to look at all the poofters taking
their baths." The man was in his mid-forties with a well-
maintained physique, a sarong wrapped around him at the
waist. "You and the missus out for a romantic stroll?"

"Don't be ridiculous," Nick snapped.[M] "Marsha is here
looking for her son, Toby, and I'm looking for my boyfriend,
Tom."

M Even though she knew it was silly (Nick was gay, she was married), the
quickness with which Nick denied being with her wounded Marsha's
pride, made her feel ever so slightly rejected, undesirable, devalued.

The man folded his arms over his chest and gave Nick an up-and-down look. "I think there are a couple of Toms down that way," he said, pointing absently along the bank, "and some Dicks and Harrys too. Try that if you want."

He turned from Nick to face Marsha: "Did your son like David Bowie?"

Marsha shook her head. "I'm not sure who he liked... you know kids and their music."

"There are a lot of hardcore Bowie fans in this area—he gave a concert here, March 7, 1987, part of the Glass Spider Tour. Anyway, a lot of us hang out with other guys who like the same celebs, you know? If you know who your son liked best, and where those fans are, you'll have a better chance of finding him. What was his name again?"

"Toby."

"I haven't met any Tobys that I can remember, sorry luv. I hope you find him though, I really do—it's the mothers who got the shit end of the stick in this whole thing. But you can bet the Author will sort it all out again." He took a step away from them, then turned back. "And you," he looked at Nick, "you should lighten up a bit. You look like one of those gay Republicans."

RICHARD AND LOUIS, in their search for Joseph, had changed tactics dramatically from when they'd first arrived and walked through the camps with Marsha. Richard was convinced they had to seek help through official government channels, get the Grimpils out of the parks in whatever way possible, get them somehow identified or sent home, or even (though the thought pained and worried him) held somewhere where loved ones could find them. Over a period of two months, the two of them had been to see the mayor of

Paris[R1] four times, but the mayor was gritty and unflinching, in her early fifties with short hair[L] swept back from
her face, and utterly unsympathetic to their concerns. She
had been controversial from the moment she took office, so
much so that her detractors had started referring to her as
Mayor Nepel.[R2] Since she claimed not to understand their
accents (Richard spoke French fluently but Louis could
barely get by), they had taken to bringing an interpreter
with them. Each time they'd asked her what she intended to
do about the thousands of foreigners who had come to her
city citing mysterious dreams and the phantom scent of carnations, all looking for the same expatriate writer that they
believed would lead or instruct or reward them for their
journey. Each time she regarded Richard and Louis coldly
and told them (through the interpreter, whose voice was
as hard and icy as the mayor's demeanour) that fools had
always come to Paris to pursue reckless dreams; that immi-
gration was a national concern and although she agreed this

R1 Héloïse Fleuriot, elected when Bertrand Delanoë's term of office ended
in 2008.

L The colour of Atlantic sand in October, when it is cold and the sand
bears just the first trace of frost.

R2 The "Nepel" epithet was in reference to the name Le Pen, specifically
the infamous Jean-Marie Le Pen, leader of the ultra-conservative Front
National and five-time presidential candidate (achieving second place
in 2002 and the oldest candidate ever to run in 2007). Héloïse Fleuriot had worked under Le Pen, and absorbed early on his intolerance
and xenophobia, using her charms and considerable intellect to refine
and intensify his views and to eventually ascend to the mayoralty of
Paris. The *International Herald Tribune* dubbed her "more Le Pen than
Le Pen" in an article covering her election, and, soon after, her detractors flipped the name and began calling her Nepel.

The Grimpils

could be considered a crisis there was nothing she could do; that police involvement was at this point not a real possibility unless they wanted to witness full-fledged riots, Parisian style, or worse—a validation of violence against these men that would lead to a vigilante mindset and citizen attacks; that the national government would have to decide how to proceed with the expulsion and handling of these invaders. She compared them to the Roma, she called them vermin, she would like nothing better than to get rid of them, but she showed no glimmer of understanding that these men were in a powerful and mysterious thrall to a hapless American author who couldn't or wouldn't help them, and ultimately she washed her hands of Richard and Louis and their concerns, every time.

THE AMERICAN EMBASSY, on Avenue Gabriel, was the only embassy in Paris Richard and Louis knew of that had fencing and armed guards. It had the air of crouching instead of standing, as though it were a child flinching from a bully.[L] Passing through security, where an unsmiling man asked for their passports and roughly patted them down, might have made less determined men turn back. But it was now August, time was taking its toll in energy and hope and ever-growing expenses. No one in their little group had turned up a loved one, nor had they heard of anyone finding or rescuing a Grimpil, and they were more desperate than ever to

---

L The concrete building extracted colour from the nearby street and storefronts, turning all of them into a uniform and hopeless grey-black, like the end-of-day water in the cup into which kindergarten children dip their paintbrushes.

make an appeal to someone in a position of power on behalf of the new lost souls of Paris.

Marsha had declined to come, preferring to continue searching the camps, clutching a picture of her son, barely stopping to shower or eat, hoping that, given enough time and perseverance, she would find him and bring him home. Nick had grown more sullen and angry with every passing day, and often refused to leave the hotel at all. So, by themselves—as they did most things now—Richard and Louis were ushered without delay past the reading room and lending library into the office of the ambassador himself.

"Gentlemen," he greeted them. "Always a pleasure to meet fellow citizens on foreign soil."

"We're Canadian." Richard had learned the French trick of speaking politely while being rude.

"Then I'm afraid you've come to the wrong embassy."

"No, no sir, I assure you, we know perfectly well where we are. We're here to talk to you about a very serious situation of which you're no doubt already aware. There are thousands of young men living without shelter in the parks and public spaces. All of these men are foreign nationals, the majority of them American."

"You mean the Grimpils."[R]

R There is a form of French slang known as Verlan, which consists of rearranging and reversing syllables. It is actively spoken in France, and several Verlan words have become so commonplace that they are used in everyday French. Simply separate the syllables, reverse them, and put a word back together again, making changes in spelling that protect the original pronunciation. "Verlan" itself is an example, a reversal of *l'envers*, French for "reverse." There are no hard and fast rules. Verlan was invented as a secret language, a way for people, notably youths, *continued overleaf . . .*

The Grimpils

"We prefer not to use that term. We feel it validates their deluded view of reality."

"Deluded?"

"What other name would you give to people who believe they were called here by the scent of carnations as they read *Dressed to the Elevens* or *Flashing the Neighbors?*" Richard began raising his voice. "What else would you call a state of mind that allowed them to leave lovers, families, jobs, entire lives? They are suffering from mass hysteria, and we need to be doing something."

"No one's coerced them. They're here of their own free will."

"Yes, but—"

"Look, your concern is touching. However, there's nothing you can do. There's nothing I can do. Have you been to see the mayor?"

"Nepel? As if she'd do anything. We've been to see her four

... *continued from p. 71*

drug users, and criminals, to communicate freely in front of authority figures. It is not surprising that it was adopted by the men who journeyed to France in search of their revered author. It was also a popular tool for creating monikers during the flurry of media attention the crisis started to receive in late spring. Every hack reporter was trying to coin a term, despite the fact the anglicized Verlan words often sounded ridiculous. Early days saw the Lersveltras, the Sencho, the Tedvode. It was an intern from an English monthly in the Czech Republic who came up with the Grimpils, a clever reversal of "pilgrims," which is what many of the men called themselves (one famously said, "I do not wish you to consider me a man; I am a pilgrim only. A pilgrim to the shrine of Paris, the city the greatest author who ever lived has chosen as his own"). The newly coined term stuck, and eventually the *New York Times* erroneously took credit. Newspaper and broadcast reporters took to using it, and "the Grimpils" caught on in the camps and among the people of Paris.

times and she keeps saying it's out of her jurisdiction." Richard was waving his arms in frustration.

"Gentlemen, please! She's a woman of action and considerable power. I'll speak to her again about this, and see what I can do."

"She won't budge, Mr. Ambassador, that's a big part of the problem," Richard said. "American citizens are suffering. Both here and back at home." Louis put his hand on Richard's shoulder. Richard took a deep breath. "If you can't help them yourself, at least plead with the writer to talk to them, to send a message, tell them it was a mistake, that he never wanted them to come here. Make him tell them all to go home."

"The writer, I'm afraid, has left Paris."

The rest of what the ambassador said—how the writer had had no choice, really, how he didn't like this kind of attention, how his boyfriend had been attacked five times by Grimpils, how they were both in hiding somewhere in the United States, how they were quite, quite *disturbed* about the whole thing—neither Richard nor Louis fully took in. Louis's fingers were squeezing Richard's shoulder, Richard's mind had tunnelled for release. While the ambassador was still explaining, the two men saw themselves out.

LOUIS'S DRINKING PROBLEM waited for him in the hotel room, the flask slipped beneath his pillow as much of a joy to him as a quarter from the tooth fairy to a child. He wanted to seek oblivion—freedom from repetitive thoughts about Joseph, about his relationship with Richard, about his increasing fascination with the Grimpils—and the only thing that could bring him that freedom was the dreamless sleep he got from drinking. He knew the habit worried Richard,

The Grimpils

hurt him even,[M] and he wanted to spare Richard that pain if he could. So he simply said he was going out for a walk.

Louis was born and raised in a small town in Ontario. While still a teenager he'd had his first sexual experience with a man, one sunset[L1] in the tobacco fields the town depended on for income. He could close his eyes and still see Tillsonburg, feel the tobacco leaves between his fingers, recall the layout of his mother's kitchen. But his whole life afterwards, in Toronto, seemed pale and distant—a dream meant to lead him here, to Paris. Walking along the Rue Saint-Antoine, catching glimpses of the Seine[L2] a couple of streets over, he wondered if that was how the Grimpils felt about their previous lives, the families and lovers they'd left behind—he wondered if they ever regretted it. If they did, they showed no sign.

He finished the flask, pocketed it, bought a bottle of Pernod at the corner of Rivoli and Renard, and continued walking towards the Bois de Boulogne. He took several deep swigs from the bottle, ignoring the stares of passersby. By the time he reached the park, he'd already drunk half of the Pernod.[L3] Some of the Grimpils who had been camping in his favourite section of the park, the area around the Moulin de Longchamp, recognized him, calling out, "Hey,

---

M Marsha had noticed how Richard would look away while Louis sipped from his flask, how he would stare at the ceiling, clenching and unclenching his jaw.

L1 Creamsicle orange and peppermint pink streaking the sky.

L2 Slate blue, reflecting the brooding clouds of late afternoon; the shade at which blue and grey become indistinguishable.

L3 A wicked absinthe-green, conspiratorial and complicit.

Louis!" and "'Jour, Louis" as he walked past, looking for a bench on which to lie down. The blackness was coming for him sooner than he'd intended, screwing up his plan to get back to the hotel just in time to pass out. He lay back on the bench and watched the Grimpils moving from tent to tent, copies of the Author's books set up in pyramids and shrines all over the grass, the Grimpils just swishing about, sashaying almost. His own hips never seemed to move like that. What must it be like to be so obviously gay, to not be able to hide it even if you wanted to? He wondered why the Author had chosen to appear to Joseph and not to him or Richard, to some gay men and not others. He wondered how Joseph was doing, wished he could be beside him right now and share this passion with him, even if it was crazy. He finished the bottle and rested his eyes on a garland of carnations hanging from a nearby branch (all Grimpils were drawn to "the Author's flower" and bought them all over the city, bringing them to the parks, lining the paths with them, decorating the trees).

All this time in Paris, and Louis had not yet paid tribute to Oscar Wilde, *his* favourite author, Wilde who had worn a green carnation as a coded sign for homosexuality. Oscar Fingal O'Flahertie Wills Wilde, who'd written *The Happy Prince,* which Louis used to read to Joseph every Christmas, making both of them cry. He shut his eyes and realized he couldn't open them again. What would Richard think about him not coming home that night, about Louis passing out in a park with the Grimpils, who felt no uncertainties?

IN LATE AUGUST, the four friends were in the Parc du Champs de Mars. Nick held a picture of Tom, Marsha had her poster of Toby, and Richard and Louis were describing

Joseph to Grimpils.[N1] Some of them started making fun of Nick's demeanour; he was acting as if he were a cop, trying to be butch—and one Grimpil actually got up and marched behind Nick, aping his rigid walk. The performance sent the other Grimpils into hysterics.

Nick turned, feral.[L1] "You think this is funny?" he shouted. "You think I'm being *funny* right now?" The man who'd parodied his walk just stood there laughing; Nick belted him in the face.

The man crumpled like a pop can,[N2] but one of his friends was instantly there to take his place. Nick was all adrenaline and fight or flight. Richard screamed at Nick to stop. Nick swung fists, kicked, even started biting. The Grimpils piled on top of him, dishing out open-handed slaps, using their fingernails to scratch, digging in with their knees and elbows. Marsha and Louis had moved away, unable to watch, staring at their shoes.[L2]

N1 Some Grimpils were dirty and reeked of body odour and sweat and dirt, but most took care of their hygiene, scented with pink grapefruit or green apple or synthetic strawberries, women's perfume, bubble gum or vanilla. With the Grimpils, it was always something sweet or fruity or feminine. Never the Old Spice that Richard wore, or the more expensive masculine colognes Louis liked, or even the Axe products Nick himself was so fond of, and never Tom's scent, that mixture of allspice and clove, almost pumpkin pie, that familiar scent Nick yearned for so badly and never smelled again.

L1 Nick's anger was stillborn blue; strangled, screaming and dead, a waste of potential.

N2 Nick could smell the man's apple-sweet saliva, the iron scent of blood.

L2 Marsha's shoes, once a bright and vibrant green, were hidden by caked-on mud and leaves the colour of dried mustard. Her pale legs were spackled with dark earth, red scabs that looked unhealthy, and some dully purple bruises.

It was Richard who ended it. He gave a young Grimpil twenty-five euros to run around to the back of the fracas and yell out, "I've just seen the Author over at Avenue Rapp and Quai d'Orsay!" The Grimpils scattered, running to catch a glimpse of their guru.

MARSHA STAYED BESIDE Nick in the hospital all morning, then Richard and Louis came to relieve her, so she could go and search for Toby. They'd arrived separately; Richard early, as usual, with a teddy bear and a balloon from the gift shop, Louis fifteen minutes late, with a bouquet of white carnations.

"Why'd you bring those?" Richard asked him. "Don't you think that's a little inappropriate?"

"They're cheap and widely available," Louis said. "I just like them."

Richard swore softly under his breath. He wished Nick hadn't gotten himself into this state: Nick's face was so swollen[M] he couldn't speak. He also wished that Marsha weren't so erratic, and that Louis weren't drinking so much, staying out all night and spending so much time with Grimpils. They were falling apart.

The last time Richard had felt so helpless and despairing had been in another hospital back in Canada, visiting Joseph, who was also recovering from a sort of fight. Joseph had always been effeminate and dramatic, such that Richard and his sister had been exchanging knowing glances since

---

M Nick lost three teeth, broke his right hand, had cuts across his knuckles, scrapes on his elbows and knees, bruised ribs, a sore kidney, and a deep gash over one eye that bled profusely, required stitches, and left an ugly scar. His head looked like a water balloon about to burst with blood and pus.

The Grimpils

the boy was barely four, glances that Richard's brother-in-law openly resented. When Joseph hit puberty, he began to wear tight clothes and bright colours. He applied shiny clear lip gloss and spent his allowance on manicures. Once his father caught him wearing smeared eyeliner[L] the morning after he'd missed his curfew, and during the huge fight that ensued Joseph told his father he was gay. The fight turned physical, leaving Joseph in the hospital with bruised ribs and a broken wrist. Richard had gone to visit Joseph immediately, and the first words out of Joseph's mouth had been to ask to come live with Richard and Louis. Richard was hesitant at first, overwhelmed, but when his sister told him she was staying with her husband, forgiving his "overreaction," he felt there was no other choice.

His sister—though clearly she'd made some bad decisions in her time—had trusted him with raising her son, and Richard had let this Grimpil debacle happen. As unpredictable and crazy as it was, he still felt responsible. And now she was trusting him to find Joseph and bring him home, helping their search by sending money every month to cover the cost of the hotel. He'd been in Paris three and a half months, with almost nothing to show for it.

TWO WEEKS AFTER Nick's fight, ten days into a thankfully warm September, a letter came for them at the hotel, from the mayor's office. It was addressed (in French) to "Citizens and foreign nationals concerned with the matter of the Grimpils" and invited them to a public address outside the Centre Georges Pompidou[R] that would detail a

---

L Soho's patented Angel Eyes, a light and shimmering blue.

R Place Georges Pompidou, 75004 Paris, +33 (0)1 44 78 12 33.

plan conceived by the municipal government (with federal approval) to deal with the matter of the Grimpils.

"It seems the mayor isn't so powerless after all," Richard said.

RICHARD AND LOUIS were worried about Marsha. Ever since the fight, they had scarcely seen her, and when they did she looked increasingly dishevelled. She had stopped washing her hair and changing her clothes, and hadn't been back to visit Nick in the hospital after that first day. She was obsessed with Toby, adamant that she could find him if only she looked hard enough, long enough.

It was ridiculous: them wandering the camps—always keeping an eye out for Joseph—looking for Marsha, who was wandering the camps to find Toby. They spent the better part of the afternoon looking. After dinner they went out again, determined to find her and tell her about the mayor's public address, to offer her some kind of hope.

The majority of family members of Grimpils who came to Paris to search for loved ones—some selling insurance policies or furniture to make the trip—were only able to stay a few days, a week. It wasn't enough time. Those who met Marsha envied her determination and persistence, asked her for advice. She had little to give. Richard tried to help them look, had even made an orientation pamphlet mapping the more permanent tent cities where different subsets of the Grimpils hung out. There were the leather daddies and the Goths and the emo kids, a whole section of drag queens. There were the fan-based camps: one for Cher, one for Madonna, Björk, and even Britney Spears (complete with still images from Chris Crocker's infamous YouTube video in her defence). Still, no one had found whom they were looking for among the tens of thousands.

The Grimpils

This night, the Grimpils seemed disturbed, a little skit-
tish—one forty-year-old Abba fan told Richard there were
rumours about people disappearing.

"Are some of you giving up on the Author and going
home?" Richard asked in a whisper of hope.

"I don't think that's it." That was all the man would say.
When Richard described Marsha to him, he pointed them
towards a distant section of the park and told them to ask
there.

The Grimpils had taken to calling her the Mater Dolo-
rosa, the sorrowful mother. Some had made sketches of
Marsha looking like the Virgin Mary and taped them up in
their makeshift shanties; some of the crueller ones laughed
at her.[M] It was eleven PM before someone pointed to a bridge
nearby and said, "She lives under there."

The place was covered in garbage, and Marsha was nes-
tled in a corner behind some cardboard, hair stringy and
wild, face dirty, eyes aglow with a crazed fire, staring at a
photograph of her son. It was the one thing she kept clean,
kept replenishing, printing and reprinting it from a scanned
photo and posting it everywhere, stapling it to telephone
poles, showing it to everyone she could.

"Marsha, honey?" Richard said. Louis hung back, afraid.
"Marsha?" He put a hand on her shoulder, but she did not
take her eyes from the photo.

As they climbed back up the bank, Louis drained his flask
and said, "She's not ever going to leave here, is she?"

[M] The laughter hurt her, yes, and made her feel ashamed, but each time it
happened it hurt a little less; slowly she was developing an immunity to
pain, a numbness she could wrap around her like a shawl.

TO GET TO the hotel, they had to walk back through the park filled with Grimpils. The scene of the Grimpils at night was wild and feline: bodies rubbing and scritching against each other in every configuration, bare flesh reflecting eerily, sinuous and fluid in the dark. They moaned, wove amongst each other, writhing and ecstatic.

Louis rose onto his toes to kiss Richard's thin lips. For Louis, it was a kiss of shared excitement at witnessing the mystery of the Grimpils and the utopia of their orgy; for Richard, it was a kiss of solace, a reminder that each of them had someone to cling to in the face of utter chaos.

THEY STOPPED FOR a drink at Le Vin de Soif, their favourite bar in Paris. They were silent, Richard lost in his own thoughts, curious about what the mayor would say the next day, Louis reading *Thicker Than Toilet Water*, trying to figure out how these comedic essays had precipitated such a reaction, how he had overlooked whatever messages the Grimpils found in them.

"Gentlemen!" Louis was so startled he dropped the book. "So lovely to see you! You're going to the address tomorrow, no doubt?"

It was the American ambassador. Richard stood to shake his hand. "Yes, Mr. Ambassador," Richard said. "You'll be there as well?"

"I knew the mayor would come through.[R] Didn't I tell you?"

[R] Tomorrow, Richard will learn the mayor found a loophole by which she enacted a legal edict originally written by a former mayor of Paris, coincidentally an ancestor of hers, Jean-Baptiste Fleuriot-Lescot, who had been mayor until July 17, 1794—during the height of the French Revolution.

The Grimpils

"You did, yes. Thank you for whatever part you had in arranging this."

"Oh, just a few phone calls. Well, I suppose I'll see you bright and early at nine! As you were!"

"Well, that's a good sign," Louis said, once the door had shut behind him.

"Yes it is." Richard smiled. He reached across the table and held his partner's hands.

LOUIS WAKES AT five AM, unable to sleep. Richard doesn't stir—Louis would have guessed he'd be awake, anxious and fretting about the morning. His own insomnia isn't from worry, exactly—it's more of an agitation, an itch, a feeling that he is supposed to be doing something else. He gets up and goes into the bathroom. On the counter is a small vase with two carnations in it. Louis had bought the white flowers before bed, after the bar, although Richard hadn't wanted him to. He had put green food colouring[L1] into the water. Now, in the early morning, the carnations have absorbed the green, letting it colour the edges of each petal. Louis removes one of the flowers and breaks the stem just below the blossom. He gets dressed and pins the flower in his lapel.

He leaves the hotel and walks quickly northeast until he comes to the gates of the Cimetière du Père-Lachaise. He doesn't need to consult the map (so many times has he studied its pathways). Oscar Wilde's gravestone is a massive granite block,[L2] flanked by art deco angels, inscribed

---

L1 The bright, generic, crayon-coloured green that children use for grass.

L2 The grey-green of deep water when the sky above is overcast and clouded.

in Greek and Latin, and wearing the lipstick kisses of hundreds of visitors, fans, and pilgrims. Louis does not know how the tradition started, but he has seen photographs of this tombstone, covered in smears of Harlot Red, Wine with Everything, Crushed Berry, Fever Shine Pixel Pink. The oldest kisses have lost their colour, remain only as oil stains in stone.

Louis kneels beside the tombstone of this author he loves, who went to jail for having a male lover, who had come to Paris and revelled in all the decadence of the city. Louis applies the lipstick he bought weeks ago,[L] rubs his lips together, feels the makeup thick and greasy, then moves forward and puts his lips against the cold grey stone.

He leans back, admires the perfect transfer. Then he turns his head sharply, alarmed by the sound of firecrackers.

MARSHA ROAMS THE Jardin des Tuileries, clutching Toby's photo. She wants to ask if somebody has seen her son, but something is wrong today. Something flits at the edge of her consciousness, but she is distracted—one car after another backfires in the nearby streets. Whatever is bothering her swoops in and quickly away again; it's gone before she can glimpse it, a sly shade creature startled by the sound of fireworks. The sun is shining, the air is warm, and the gardens are beautiful, though the grass and flowers are trampled and bare in patches, worn by heavy traffic. It really is odd: there is no one there to ask about Toby.

Dark stains clot in the gravel pathways, paint or spilled red wine. She hears the churning gears of heavy trucks, the sound of distant screams. Richard is running towards her

---

L Garrulous Green, from Lancôme.

The Grimpils

now, calling out, but Marsha barely hears him. She is shivering, suddenly as cold as that night in Toby's room last fall. In her mind's eye she is once again lowering the sheet over him, but this time he's not sleeping and she covers his face with it. Richard splays beside her on the grass, arms reaching out, sobbing something she can't hear—her ears are filled with the whirrs and electric hiccoughs of the supercomputer that calculates danger, waiting for it to tell her how this happened, to tell her what it is that she's forgotten to do to save her son.[M]

THE RENEGADE
ANGELS OF PARKDALE

"**W**hat are you doing tonight?"

"Nothing," Zach said. There was a pause. "Watching season three of *The Golden Girls* and eating an entire tub of ice cream."

"Wrong." Lucky made that annoying buzzer sound he always did. "And P.S., you sound like a pregnant lesbian."

"Well, thanks for calling."

"Look, the DVDs will be there when you get home. You've got to leave that apartment sometime."

"I go to work," Zach said.

"I mean leave the house for *fun*. Go out. Do something."

"I'm not ready yet. I don't feel fun."

"Listen, Zach. I'm going to Fallen tonight, and you're coming with me."

"Lucky."

"Don't even start. You're coming, even if I have to come over there and drag you out. Trust me: this is the coolest gay dance night in the city and you need to get out of the house and shake your boo-tay."

Zach sighed. "Where's Fallen?"

"It used to be Stone's Place. Angels own it now."

"Like, Hell's Angels?"

"No, like, the renegade angels of Parkdale."

Zach thought maybe it was a band he hadn't heard of. Was that really all it took to be the hippest thing in town? A band-themed bar changes ownership and becomes another band-themed bar, different signed pictures in the same old frames? He wished people would just leave well enough alone—allow people to form their attachments without always trying to renovate and improve them. Facebook had already changed its interface three times in the seven months since he'd lost Dan. Why? What was the point?

"Fine. I'll meet you at Dufferin Station at nine-thirty," Zach said.

"Ten-thirty. Nobody gets there before eleven."

"Fine. But I'm still eating all of this ice cream."

"Fine."

LUCKY HUNG UP the phone and dialled Logan. He got his voice mail.

"Logan, buddy—Fallen tonight. Miracle of miracles, I actually convinced Zach to come out. So be there—it'll be his first time out since you-know-what, so I'm going to need your help making sure he's OK. Plus, this is going to be the best dance night since the heyday of Big Primpin'. Be there for 11."

He hung up and spent a few minutes texting guys he'd been talking to online, asking if they were going to be there. Then he arranged dinner with another friend, and got in the shower to get ready.

AS THE DUFFERIN bus chugged south, past the mall and the park, Zach had to re-evaluate his thinking. The renegade angels of Parkdale, Lucky told him, were not a band at all. They were actual angels—heavenly creatures—who had abandoned their posts and come down to Earth, ostensibly to party.

"It's been popular for a while now," Lucky said. "They have angel bars in Brooklyn—Williamsburg—and in the Seventh Ward of New Orleans, the Haight in San Francisco. They're all over Europe, too: Berlin, Paris, Amsterdam. Sometimes I swear it's like you live under a rock."

"I've had a lot on my mind," Zach said. "They're not going to push religion on me, are they? Convince me to go to church?"

"No, dumb-ass," Lucky said. "It's not like that. These are angels who were fed up with the way things were, decided to have some fun. This blog I was reading said that the angels are spiritual, not religious. Whatever that means."

Zach groaned. "You know I don't like that stuff. There's no scientific evidence for spirit."

"It's a dance party, not a meditation group," Lucky said. "Relax."

THEY GOT OFF the bus at Queen Street and turned away from the Gladstone, heading under the train bridge and entering Parkdale. They were quiet, taking it in, adjusting to the new energy. There was something scattered and untidy about Parkdale, something jittery, uninhibited and bold, and it was that way long before the angels had arrived. Parkdale seethed, breathed, craved. Parkdale shivered, shimmered, bent the light. Parkdale let everyone in: no gatekeepers, no guards, no one barring the way.

Once, five years ago, Zach was leaving Dan's Parkdale apartment, the one on Leopold, still hungover and on his way to work. It was a walk of shame; he left the building

The Renegade Angels of Parkdale

unshowered and stinky, teeth unbrushed, and ducked into a Coffee Time for some quick black freedom. He couldn't wait to have his first sip, he needed it so badly, so he opened the little plastic flap at the counter, praised Christ when the weird little holder button actually caught, had his sip and burned his taste buds off—totally worth it. But as he stepped out, struggling with the door, a bit of scalding coffee splashed out and onto his thumb, making him drop the whole thing *and* the change he was holding in his other hand. That feeling, as he watched his coffee stream out onto the sidewalk at the same time he realized the burn on his thumb was fine, it wasn't *anything*, his skin wasn't even red, as he heard his coins scurry away, already rolling and shoring up against the legs of a passed-out homeless man, as his headache knocked unanswered inside his head—that mixed-up feeling of frustration, tragicomic accident, nearly missed relief—that feeling was Parkdale.

Or had been. Now, walking through Parkdale for Zach was like walking through a mausoleum; everything felt memorial and imbued with significance. There was the corner where he and Dan had first kissed. There the bar where they'd celebrated Zach's twenty-eighth birthday, when Dan had given him a Rolex watch—which he couldn't stand to wear, now. Up the street, the burger spot where they'd first talked about living together. Now he was passing the twenty-four-hour pizza spot he and Dan had grabbed late night slices at more times than he could remember. Even just walking down the sidewalk with Lucky prattling on felt wrong—why wasn't Dan bobbing along beside them, making his dry jokes? How could he just be *gone?*

AS THEY WALKED the short distance to the bar, Lucky thought about how angels the world over always chose the neighbourhoods that were gently resisting gentrification, the places where the students and artists and homos and lower-income families all congregated, along with the sketchy, the drug-addled, and the insane. Lucky had spent many a morning in Parkdale after wild nights taking obscene quantities of MDMA, comforted that unlike in his own neighbourhood, where mothers and nannies with strollers would scowl at his wide starry pupils and spandex clothes, in Parkdale no one would even notice—every second doorway held some shaky strung-out person coming down. The angels, Lucky figured, knew how Parkdale worked. They were trying to preserve the neighbourhood's character, keep it from the yoga studios and fancy cafés and bars with velvet ropes, bouncers, and bottle service. They knew what it was to be outcast, searching for a home, and what it was to spend time in the margins, between worlds.

"WELCOME TO FALLEN," Lucky said, as they got in the line that was stretching out past the Rhino. "I missed the opener because I was at Lovers and Losers with Steve. Cody was here though, and he said it was off the hook. This is going to rock. Doesn't it feel good to be out?"

Zach gave a noncommittal grunt for an answer. Nothing had felt good to him for a long time. People were always telling him that he should move, that remaining in the apartment he and Dan had shared was unhealthy, too many reminders. They missed the fact that the alternative to being reminded—forgetting—was unthinkable to him. And Zach had grown used to the memories in that place, walking among them, reliving the past without having to replace it with anything new. Half the time he could delude himself that Dan was simply out, at work or running some errand, perpetually just about to walk through the front door. Zach

The Renegade Angels of Parkdale

was unconvinced that being out in the world was somehow qualitatively better than sitting around at home: he was going to be miserable either way, and at least at home it was a misery he was used to. Being out, in Parkdale, around normal people blissfully untouched by death, happy couples who thought they had forever together—it hurt in a different way. He hadn't wanted to come, but he simply hadn't had the energy to resist Lucky's exhortations.

As they got closer to the front, they could see an angel standing by the door, and a guy in a pageboy cap who looked about twenty seated in a chair beside him, writing on a yellow legal pad. The angel was tall—Zach guessed seven feet—with short-cropped chestnut hair. The angel's face was disfigured, a vicious scar stretching from his upper lip to his right ear, thick and raised like a shiny pink rope. Zach pictured Biblical battles, angels throwing each other out of Heaven in great wars, and shuddered.

"I was expecting wings," he whispered to Lucky. The guys in front of them overheard and the taller one turned with a snide look on his face.

"Wings only appear when an angel is in flight," he chided. "This must be your first time." He looked disgusted and turned back to his friend, who snickered into his hand.

"He wasn't talking to you," Lucky said. "And *you* better not be laughing at *us*."

Both guys turned away, and after a couple minutes said something to the angel, who let them by. The angel turned to address the line, with Lucky and Zach standing at the front.

"Listen up," he said. "The admittance policy at Fallen is as follows: E.E.L.S. or Squeals. If you pick E.E.L.S., you must cry out *Eli, Eli, lama sabachthani* as loud as you can. If you pick Squeals, you must tell me the moment in your life in which you experienced the most profound despair. Otherwise you don't get in."

"Why should I scream something if I don't know what it means?" Zach asked.

"It means *My God, My God, why have you abandoned me?*" the angel said. "They were the final words of Jesus as He died on the cross." Then he lowered his voice to a conspiratorial whisper, drawing his finger across his scar: "To be honest, it's more Lucifer's bag than any of the rest of ours, but Metatron insisted."

"Good enough for me," Lucky said. And then he yelled, "Eli, Eli, lama sabachthani!"

"Very good," the angel said. "You may pass." The guy in the chair scribbled on the legal pad.

Zach took a deep breath and looked the angel in the eyes. "My boyfriend Dan killed himself in the bathtub while I was watching TV in our living room."

"You may pass," the angel said. "But first you must serve as scribe."

"Excuse me?"

"Great," the seated guy said, getting up. "I was getting worried I was going to be out here forever. Don't worry; it's easy, and kind of fun. It's like a live version of FML."

"What's FML?" Zach asked.

"Oh my God," Lucky said. "You're hopeless. Fuck My Life? It's the best website ever—people post all the horrible things that happen to them, and you can vote whether you agree the person's life sucks or tell them they deserved it. Anyway, do you think you can handle this?"

"Yeah, I'll be fine."

"OK then. I'm going to go inside. I'll come check on you in a bit."

The Renegade Angels of Parkdale

"Whatever," Zach said. Lucky held the door open for the former scribe and went inside.

"It's not a job to be taken lightly," the angel said. "Records are important to angels. You have to write down what each person says as they come in, but no names."

"And what exactly do you do?"

"You've heard the expression *from your lips to God's ears?*" Zach nodded. "I'm the angel who makes sure those messages get delivered."

"Eli, Eli, lama sabachthani!"

"Eli, Eli, lama sabachthani!"

"Eli, Eli, lama sabachthani!"

"My mother died of a stroke the day before my wedding."

"Eli, Eli, lama sabachthani!"

"My parents kicked me out of the house when I told them that I was gay."

"Eli, Eli, lama sabachthani!"

"My father fell off of an eight-foot ladder and landed on his face, which destroyed his teeth and glasses. He broke both hands and a wrist bone was sticking out of his arm. I was the one who found

"So, how long were you out there for?" Lucky asked the former scribe.

"Just about ten minutes, really," he said, "but someone else told me that last month he sat out there the whole night and never got let in."

"Shit, I hope that doesn't happen to Zach."

"Oh my God," the scribe said, clutching Lucky's arm, "Those three guys over there are from *1 Girl 5 Gays* on MTV! I have to go get a picture!"

"Whatever," Lucky said. "Try not to drool on them."

LUCKY WENT AND got a couple of beers. He looked around the club. He could tell which guys were the angels, he thought, mostly by their height. But there him, and I was only fourteen years old."

"Eli, Eli, lama sabachthani!"

"My favourite uncle just got convicted of abusing the girls on the hockey team he used to coach."

"The first time I started using again after being sober for eight months."

"My best friend lethally overdosed on drugs that I had sold him. I never told the family."

"Eli, Eli, lama sabachthani!"

"I was diagnosed with terminal ovarian cancer at twenty-eight."

"When I told my dad I was gay he told me that he'd been cheating on my mom with men for years, and that I should marry a woman anyway."

"Eli, Eli, lama sabachthani!"

"Eli, Eli, lama sabachthani!"

"Eli, Eli, lama sabachthani!"

were tall human dudes too, and some short angels, so sometimes it took a second for him to figure it out. He focused on the music, his favourite kind to dance to: a mixture of pop hits and club classics and deliciously retro soul and R&B anthems. It was going to be a good night.

LUCKY'S FRIEND Jason spotted him from the dance floor and made his way through the crowd to say hi. He had sweat on his brow and wet stains in the armpits of his deep V t-shirt.

"Lucky!" he yelled over the music. "This party is awesome! These angels know how to dance. Have you noticed how hot they are? All muscles and scars and tall to boot. Delicious!"

"How could I miss it?"

"You think we can sleep with them? Like, physically, I mean?"

"Man, I don't even know what they're made of. But don't people sleep with them in the Bible? Or, you know, that story about the guy who wrestles with the angel? Closeted religious guys always love that story, get turned on."

The Renegade Angels of Parkdale

"It's a tie between the moment I found out I was HIV positive and the first time I lied about it to a partner."

"Eli, Eli, lama sabachthani!"

"Eli, Eli, lama sabachthani!"

"Eli, Eli, lama sabachthani!"

"I cheated on the LSAT test and never got caught."

"Eli, Eli, lama sabachthani!"

"I don't know, man. My parents are atheists. I didn't grow up believing any of this stuff." He ran his finger under his nose. "I'm going to go do a bump in the bathroom, wanna come?"

"No, I'm gonna go for a smoke and check on my friend. I'll catch up with you later."

"Cool, dude. See ya."

ON HIS WAY OUT, Lucky ran into a promoter he knew from Yes Yes Y'all.

"You don't think is better than my party, do you?"

"Hell, yes," Lucky said.

Lucky walked out the door and fished for his smokes.

"Zach," he said, "how's it going?"

"This is excruciating. I hate you for bringing me here."

"Listen man," Lucky put his hand on the angel's shoulder, "can my buddy be done here now? I think he's had enough. Help me out."

"Are you willing to take his place?" the angel asked.

"Um, can I do it later? I was kind of keen on us both being inside, at the party, together. Is that too much to ask?"

The angel looked at Zach for a long time. The people in line grew quiet. Finally he spoke.

"You've served your time," he said. "You may pass. Enjoy." He turned to Lucky. "An angel will summon you when it is your time to serve as scribe. Be ready." Then he turned to the next person in line. "You're up," he said. "E.E.L.S. or

Squeals, and you can begin your duty as scribe by writing down your own response."

"Let's go," Lucky said, and he grabbed Zach's arm and led him inside.

INSIDE, ZACH WANTED a drink immediately. He went to the bar at the back of the room, rather than the one right by the dance floor, which was impossibly busy. As he waited his turn, he looked around the room. Who were all these people? Where did they come from? Were they really having as much fun as they seemed to be?

As his eyes adjusted to the dimness, he noticed something odd about the angels. Not only were they very tall, many of them bearing visible scars, but they also gave off a faint light. They were glowing—not like a spotlight was on them, not the way children's toys glow greenish in the dark, but an internal glow, like pregnant women are said to have. They looked exceedingly healthy, all of them, flushed and bearing a slight sheen of sweat. But the light itself came from inside, Zach thought. It was as though they were animated not by the same spark of life that moved animals and humans, but by the very Light of Heaven. Their cells shone.

The guy in front of him turned away from the bar, drinks in hand. Zach smiled at him. "Have you noticed that the angels glow?"

"Yeah," the guy said. "It creeps me out. It reminds me of those skin lampshades from the Holocaust."

Zach placed his order and put his cash down on the counter. He took his drinks without waiting for change.

Lucky was smiling at him when he got back. "That guy in the yellow t-shirt was totally checking you out while you were at the bar," he said. "You should go for it."

The Renegade Angels of Parkdale

"Whatever." Zach waved his hand dismissively, not even looking.

"Well, suit yourself," Lucky said. "I have to find Logan. He's supposed to be here. You want to come or you want to wait here?"

Zach motioned that he would wait. Lucky took off.

LUCKY FOUND LOGAN standing on the stairs in the back, waiting in the long line that had developed for the downstairs washrooms.

"Hey man! God, the least they could have done was renovate this, or change the layout," Lucky said. "The washrooms here have always been the worst."

Logan didn't say anything. He was leaning against the wall, smiling.

"You're already high, aren't you?" Lucky accused. Logan grinned, nodded. They stood there a couple minutes, waiting to move forward. "This line sucks—I don't want to leave Zach for too long. Why don't we just go pee outside?"

"I don't really have to go," Logan said. "I just want to powder my nose."

"Ten-four," Lucky said. "Let's get so high we never come down."

ZACH, LEFT ON his own, watched the crowd for a bit. Invariably now, on the rare occasions he left the apartment for something other than work, his mind played tricks on him, making him think he saw Dan. Once, early on, he'd yelled at a random businessman with Dan's neat haircut and navy pea coat: "Why did you do it?" The man hadn't even stopped walking, having no idea Zach was shouting at him specifically. Tonight was no different: scanning the crowd of men, he'd see Dan out of the corner of his eye and snap his head to look—a reflex he couldn't help, no matter how many times it happened. Of course, Dan was never there, just some stranger who vaguely, superficially resembled him.

The crowd parted and he saw Dan walking towards him. He knew it couldn't be true, and yet he froze, staring—until the man got closer and Zach realized he was too short, had the wrong nose, eyes too far apart—looked nothing like Dan, really, but moved with his bouncy gait. Zach felt he could go crazy just standing there. He needed to find someone to talk to.

He recognized a bald man standing a few feet over. Zach tapped him on the shoulder. He blinked at Zach from behind his glasses.

"I don't know if this is against the rules or whatever," Zach said, "but I just wanted to say that I'm really sorry about your father."

"What?"

Zach leaned in close to his ear. "Your father," he said, "his accident. I was the scribe outside when you came in. I just wanted to say I'm sorry."

"Fuck you!" the man yelled. "You don't know me! Get out of my face!" He huffed off, leaving Zach alone.

WHEN LUCKY AND Logan stumbled back up the stairs and rejoined the party, they could see Zach pulling typical wallflower moves. He was standing with a view of the dance floor but far enough from it that no one watching would think he was trying to dance, and no one dancing would grab him and drag him in. Lucky noticed the yellow t-shirt guy standing not too far from Zach, looking at him. Zach was scanning the dancing crowd, jerking his head around in a weird way. When he finally saw them, he waved.

The Renegade Angels of Parkdale

98

"I think Zach has a stalker," Lucky said, "and he's fucking cute. Let's get that boy on the dance floor and see if we can get them together."

"For sure," said Logan.

When they stepped forward, Lucky was stopped by two firm hands on each of his shoulders.

"You are called," the first angel said. "It is your time to serve as scribe."

"Can I go after this song?" Lucky quipped. "I was just about to get my dance on."

"It is no trivial thing to be beholden to an angel," the second angel said. "You promised you would serve when your time came. That time is now. No excuses."

"OK, OK," Lucky said, shaking their hands off his shoulders. "I'm coming. Logan, tell Zach what's up, OK?"

"Sure thing, dude."

"Alright angels, lead the way." Lucky walked through the crowd between the preternaturally tall angels, the one in front clearing the way and the one behind making sure he followed.

When they got outside Lucky clapped the back of the red-haired youth sitting in the chair. He was wearing a tank top, revealing pale shoulders covered with constellations of freckles.

"You're all done, Ginger," Lucky said. "I'm driving now." Lucky took his place, the pad, and the flimsy pen that had come from a coffee shop down the street. "Hey Scarface," Lucky said, "are you sure you can read my chicken scratch? I'm pretty ripped, and I'm worse than a doctor at the best of times."

The bouncer angel didn't even smile. "Just write."

"Ten-four," Lucky said. "Loud and clear."

"Lucky's got to do his scribe thing now," Logan said.

"No worries!" yelled Zach.

"Are you OK?" Logan asked.

"Fine!" Zach answered. People always asked him that now, and his answer was always the same.

"Having fun?"

"More or less!"

"I'm going to go dance—you should come with me!"

"No, man. I'm good right here."

"Come on!" Logan pouted. "Dance with me!"

"Bathroom," Zach lied. He drained his beer and headed to the back stairs.

THE WASHROOMS were as disgusting as Zach remembered. Water covered the entire floor, though it was unclear exactly where it came from; the toilet stalls were on a raised part of the floor, and neither one seemed clogged. One of the sinks had wadded-up toilet paper blocking the drain and was full. Zach waited his turn for the urinals, staring at his distorted reflection in the rippling water on the floor.

"Eli, Eli, lama sabachthani!"

"Eli, Eli, lama sabachthani!"

"Eli, Eli, lama sabachthani!"

"When I realized that I was too much of a coward to stand up to my boss who yells at me for no reason."

"When I failed to qualify for the Olympics for the third and final time."

"Eli, Eli, lama sabachthani!"

"My Visa information got stolen by a corrupt porn site and I ended up losing my car and my apartment."

"Eli, Eli, lama sabachthani!"

"Eli, Eli, lama sabachthani!"

"Eli, Eli, lama sabachthani!"

"My father's feet got amputated in an elevator accident on Easter."

"Eli, Eli, lama sabachthani!"

The Renegade Angels of Parkdale

He did his business, then waited even longer to wash his hands. He sang "Happy Birthday" to himself while he washed them, to make sure he killed all the germs—Dan had taught him that, and now it was habit, and Dan was gone. No one in the bathroom spoke to Zach or made eye contact with him in the mirror, which suited him just fine. Guys were entering the stalls in twos and threes.

He wished he were at home, alone, far from all of this. He went upstairs planning to leave.

"Eli, Eli, lama sabachthani!"

"Eli, Eli, lama sabachthani!"

"When I accidentally ran over my neighbour's dog with my car."

"Eli, Eli, lama sabachthani!"

"When I cheated on my boyfriend for the first time."

"Eli, Eli, lama sabachthani!"

"You are finished now," the angel told Lucky. "Your service is over."

"I was just getting used to this," Lucky said. "But I'm not going to argue."

He got off the chair, had a smoke, then went back inside. He couldn't see Zach anywhere, but Logan was coming off the dance floor and going for a drink. Lucky came up beside him.

"You done already?" Logan asked. "That was only, like, three songs."

"I don't really get the way they time it," Lucky said. "I heard last month some guy had to sit out there the whole night. Where's Zach?"

"Bathroom," Logan said. "But he should be back any minute now."

"Did he talk to that platinum blonde in the t-shirt yet?"

"I don't think so. He keeps standing around or just taking off for the bathroom."

"Fuck. Let's go look for him."

BY THE TIME Lucky and Logan found him again at the back of the bar, Zach was standing with Paul, someone Dan used to work with, whom Zach hadn't seen since the funeral.

"Paul, you remember Lucky and Logan?"

"Of course. Good to see you guys." Lucky and Logan just bobbled their heads on their necks.

"Hey, do they have food here?" Paul asked. "I want nachos. I'm fucking starved."

"I don't think there's a kitchen," Zach said. The bar was all couches and garage sale chairs and mismatched dusty floor lamps. Zach thought either the angels were lazy and hadn't been bothered to change things much, or else they just wanted it to look like a bohemian apartment—second-hand furniture, mismatched glasses, everything a little bit used looking.

Just as he was about to suggest getting out of there to grab some food—Poutini's, maybe—and go home, an angel came over with a plate piled with flat pastries that looked like a cross between tea biscuits and rice cakes.

"It's not nachos," the angel said, "but maybe it will do?"

"What is it?" Logan asked.

"It is manna," the angel said. "The food of heaven."

"No offence," Paul said, "But is there a kitchen? Do you, like, have a menu?"

"No," the angel said. "No menu, no kitchen. Please, try it."

Zach took one of the thin cakes from the tray. It was made from some kind of flour he didn't recognize, the colour of coriander seeds. He bit into it. It crumbled in his mouth, and tasted sweet like honey. Almost immediately his hunger vanished.

"It's delicious," Paul said, chewing his with his mouth open. "Do we have to, like, pay you for it?"

The angel smiled. "You do not. This is just what I do. In the Bible, I was the angel who carried the prophet Habakkuk to bring food to Daniel in the lion's den. I'm the angel that brings food to the hungry."

"I think you missed a few million," Zach said. "They could probably use you in sub-Saharan Africa."

"Your sarcasm serves no one," the angel said. "God does not allow me to bring food to those people."

"But He lets you bring it to us?" Zach asked. "What makes us so special?"

The angel shook his head. "Giving you this food does not greatly change your lot in life, the course you're on. We renegades can bend the rules, break some if we're careful, but we can't affect change on a global scale. I would if I could. You have no idea."

"I'm sorry," Zach said.

"Is that why you're a renegade angel?" asked Paul. "So you can bend God's rules?"

The angel sighed. "Each angel's reasons are his own. I have always served God, and still do, in my way. But I tired of being invisible, merely suggesting things to people without them ever knowing I existed. Sometimes, it's nice to be seen."

"I hear that," Logan said.

"When we are not in this world, angels are divided: those who followed Lucifer when he was expelled, and those still in Heaven. But this place is neutral. Here, angels from both sides can gather to enjoy ourselves and forget our past."

"Must be nice," Zach said.

The angel didn't answer.

"Well, anyway, thanks for the food," Lucky said.

"You are most welcome, each of you," said the angel. He moved on, offering the manna cakes to other guys throughout the bar, all of whom grabbed at them greedily.

THERE WERE photographers at the party, walking around taking candid shots of everyone and passing out their business cards with websites printed on them. Zach tried to avoid their lenses. There was a photo booth—poached from the Business Woman's Special party, according to Logan, from Chronologic, according to Paul—where people could pose in front of different backgrounds. They had their pictures taken, these partiers, to post them to their Facebook profiles. Their real-time image one night became the online avatar they hid behind the next, showing they were there, proving they had fun, looked good, made friends.

Logan, Lucky, and Paul headed for the dance floor, begging Zach to come. He refused, but only after they made him promise not to leave until they got back.

His three friends charged into the smoke and lights, Logan ripping his shirt off and tucking it into his pants as he walked. They danced wildly, letting the music take them over. Zach watched from his place on the sidelines.

An angel approached him then, almost eight feet tall, wearing an eye patch.

"Does it ever seem pointless?" Zach asked.

"What?"

"All this. I mean, not just this bar, this night, but all of it? Life, I guess."

The angel looked at him blankly.

The Renegade Angels of Parkdale

"Creation, maybe. The universe. I'm not good with New Age stuff—I was a science major."

"Science is as good a path to God as any," the angel said.

"Whatever," Zach said. "But I mean, are you happy to be an angel? Just carrying messages from one person to another, not knowing if they'll listen, or if your message will ease their pain? Is that enough for you?"

"It's what I am," the angel said, "and message carrying is very important work, vital. Look." Here he held out his hand, and Zach shook it.

Zach didn't close his eyes, but his view of the room around him fell away, and he could see what he knew was his own body, on a microscopic level. He saw the electricity in his brain, flying between neurons, constantly building, reinforcing, and connecting neural pathways; the way other signals were coursing between his body and his brain; he felt the weight of his clothes against his skin, his own body weight and gravity against his feet in his shoes, the smells of the bar, the residual taste of the manna in his mouth. All these physical sensations translated into sparks of light and energy conducted along specific structures of his biology designed solely for this purpose. He could see the functioning of his cells, the way epigenetic markers told specific sequences of his DNA what to do, and how the DNA in turn told the cells what to do: how to repair themselves, reproduce themselves, how to differentiate themselves from one another to strengthen and heal his body. He saw how his thoughts and emotions sent signals to various endocrine glands, how each emotion could be reduced to the production of certain chemical enzymes, whose physical properties interacted with each other and with the tissues of his body.

The angel let go of Zach's hand, and the vision vanished.

"You see?" the angel asked. "Angels are those sparks of electricity inside your body, but on a universal scale. Life is simply messages, from one place to another and back again."

"I'm just not sure that life is worth all that effort," Zach said. "Life for the sake of itself—I don't get it."

"Maybe you don't need to," the angel said. Zach rolled his eyes.

"Can I ask you one more thing?"

"Certainly," the angel said.

"Can you go to, like, the other side or whatever? I mean, can you talk to dead people?"

"Angels speak to human souls," the angel said, "whether they are in living bodies or not."

"I just want to know if Dan is alright. That he's, you know, OK wherever he is. Happy."

"He's where he needs to be," the angel said.

"That's it?"

"That's all there is to say."

"Thanks for nothing," Zach said. He turned his back to the angel and strode away.

MARVELLING AT THE vision of his body and wanting to flee the angel who'd given it to him, Zach joined Lucky and Logan on the dance floor, still slightly shaken. It had been over a year since he'd been out dancing. He forgot how, at first—shifted his weight awkwardly from one foot to the other, held his hands in fists at his hips, barely moving. He kept looking at the guys in the crowd—everyone sweaty, seemingly blissful. But how could they be? There was the drug dealer who'd killed his friend, there the perpetrator of a hit-and-run, there a young woman with terminal cancer. What did they have to dance about? Zach inched his way across the floor until he was close enough to Lucky to scream in his ear. But Lucky saw him first.

"This DJ is amazing! It's Seraphiel, the angel of song!"

Zach looked over at the booth and saw an eight-foot angel wearing a tight red t-shirt that said I ♥ YHWH on it. When he took his headphones off to change a track, Zach saw that one of his ears was missing, a nasty snarl of scar tissue in its place.

"How can you do it?" he screamed at Lucky. "How can you dance when you know how sad these people are?"

"Stop using your brain!" Lucky screamed. "You're not fucked up enough. Take some drugs!"

Zach shook his head; he didn't want to try that stuff. His moods were volatile enough without adding artificial doses of dopamine or serotonin or whatever it was that drugs gave you into the mix. He started to walk off the dance floor. He didn't know what to do out there, how to pretend that nothing was wrong with his life and flail around. He went and sat on one of the empty couches to sulk.

LUCKY WENT BACK to Logan on the dance floor, noticeably upset.

"Why won't he dance?" he screamed at Logan. "He's got to get out of this funk!"

"Give him time!" Logan yelled back, gyrating in a tight circle.

"It's been almost a year!"

"Maybe that's not enough. He's fine. Just dance!"

Lucky danced a bit, considering Logan's words. But he was soon distracted by a gym bunny in a tank top who was leering at him while he danced. Lucky went over to him, threw his arms around his neck, and started grinding his pelvis into the body builder's. The guy grabbed at his ass in a rough way Lucky didn't like, so he broke it off and moved back to where Logan was spinning around in the same small circle.

"Look!" Logan said. He put one arm around Lucky and pointed with the other. "Yellow t-shirt finally made his move!" Zach was chatting with him on the couch.

"Thank God!" Lucky said. "Let's hope they hook up. That boy needs to get laid!"

ZACH WAS LOOKING at the floor when he felt someone sit down on the couch beside him. He looked over to see a guy about his age with fine, white-blond hair and sky blue eyes, wearing a t-shirt the colour of hard-boiled egg yolk, adorned with a cartoon duck.

"I'm Alar," he said.

"Zach." They shook hands. "Are you an angel?"

Alar sprayed a mouthful of beer. "No!" he guffawed. "I'm an Estonian. And a very, very, drunk one at that." He laughed again, so hard he snorted like a pig.

"Well, here's to that," Zach said. They clinked beer bottles.

"No, seriously, thanks for the compliment," Alar managed when he finally swallowed. "Those angels are hot. I can't believe you would mistake me for one of them." He gestured at a group of three angels talking nearby, all tall, handsome despite their scars, and faintly glowing.

"It's just an unusual name, is all," Zach explained. "Like one of theirs. First time here?"

"No, second."

"E.E.L.S. or Squeals?"

"Squeals. Both times. My Aramaic is shit."

They took sips of their drinks.

"I'm curious," Zach said. "Did you say the same thing both times?"

"What?"

"Was your Squeal the same? The same moment of greatest despair?"

Alar's gaze hardened. "Nope," he said. "Life sucks that way—whatever the worst thing is that ever happened to you, whatever it is that you think maybe, just maybe, you've survived, you'll never know for sure that something even worse isn't going to happen to you tomorrow."

Zach contemplated that. Something worse than Dan's death—was it possible? Almost at once he realized it was, and felt a new plummet of despair. He wanted to ask Alar what his two Squeals had been, but they were both distracted by a loud sound, that of cloth tearing.

THE MUSIC ON the dance floor stopped. Lucky was facing away from the crowd, clinging to a thin college student with his tongue down his throat.

"Hey," he said, turning towards the DJ's booth, "what gives?"

"Holy shit," the student said. "What the fuck?" He pointed at the closest angel.

"Ascension time," a girl beside them said. "Hold on to your hats." The clothes ripped off of the angels' bodies. In unison, their shirts split open as their wings erupted forth: giant, feathered, majestic wings that sprung from their backs, extended above their shoulders, and brushed the floor with their tips. They had the beauty of swans' wings but looked as powerful and regal as eagles'. The wings did not flap, but their feathers rustled and moved, and the people on the dance floor felt a breeze across their faces, a gathering of wind. The angles were naked now, leaving pants and belts and ripped shirts in piles beneath them and raising themselves up, glowing so brightly that the details of their bodies could not be seen, though the light was not painful to look at. They rose as one flock, and then they passed through the ceiling, leaving everyone behind.

As soon as the last wingtip disappeared—silently, effortlessly—the house lights came on, casting everyone in a harsh fluorescence. Men who had seemed mysterious and attractive just moments before now looked tired, pathetic, and wasted. The manna left on platters across the bar turned to ash, which swirled in the eddies of air left behind by the angels' flight.

"That's it," a burly man called from behind the bar. "Everybody out!"

ZACH WALKED OUT of Fallen beside Alar, who was weaving unsteadily. He was drunker than Zach had realized. He didn't really have anything to say, yet they had just witnessed something miraculous together, and perhaps had been on the brink of sharing. It seemed inappropriate to Zach to walk away without at least some kind of goodbye.

When they got outside, they drifted a little bit west of the entrance. Guys were piling out behind them, everyone crowding the sidewalk to hail cabs, light smokes, and wait for their friends. Alar turned and looked at Zach with bleary eyes.

"Well, I'm this way," Zach said. He gestured down the street. "Dufferin."

"I'm west," Alar said.

The Renegade Angels of Parkdale

They faced each other, seemingly with nothing else to say. "Well, it was nice to meet you," Alar giggled.

Zach moved in for a quick hug, but felt Alar's open mouth sliding wetly around his neck and ear. Zach was surprised, and uncomfortable, but already his neck was tingling where Alar's mouth was, prickling shoots rising up into the back of his skull and down the length of his side. He breathed in, smelling the sweat in Alar's hair: booze sweet, but clean underneath, like a baby's. He gasped, realized he was already half erect. He moaned without meaning to and felt embarrassed. He tightened his hug, pressed Alar against him, squeezed. Then, without warning, the thought of Dan near eviscerated him with cold shock. He could not hold Dan like this, not ever again. He missed the shape of Dan's body, those familiar contours, and suddenly this stranger in his arms felt foreign and wrong. He let go and they broke apart awkwardly.

They looked at each other: one blushing, one reeling.

"Oops," Alar said. Then he spun around and smacked into a parked car, setting off the alarm.

"My God, are you OK?"

"Oh my God. No. Oh my God. I have to hurl." Alar crouched down on the curb and began vomiting noisily into the street.

LUCKY CAME TUMBLING out of the bar with Logan and four other guys they'd been talking to on the dance floor. Lucky was sure that the college student and at least one of the other guys wanted to sleep with him, and was pretty confident he could work it into a threesome. Despite the fact that all the guys spilling out of the bar were trying to flag down cabs, causing congestion in the single lane of eastbound traffic,

Lucky held up his hand and whistled and managed to snare a van cab right away. He gestured Logan into it and went over to say goodbye to Zach.

"Zach baby! We're going to Après Boum to keep this bitch going. Maybe Comfort Zone, too. You wanna come?"

"No way. I'm done. Going home."

"Where'd your new friend go?" Lucky raised his eyebrows. Zach motioned towards Alar, prostate and puking on the curb beside the screaming car. "Nice," Lucky said. "That's the sign of a good night. You into him?"

Zach shrugged.

Lucky looked his friend in the eyes. "At least tell me you had fun," he said. "Please tell me it was worth me dragging you out here."

"It wasn't bad."

"It was awesome," Lucky said. "I'm glad you came." He glanced back at the cab. "OK, gotta run. I've got two warming up in there, wouldn't do to leave them alone. Wish me luck!" He kissed Zach on both cheeks and climbed into the van. It honked as it drove off.

ZACH LOOKED BACK at Alar, who was standing again.

"Are you OK man? How much did you drink?"

"This was supposed to be a fun night for me. Enjoy life. Forget my troubles."

"How did that work out for you?"

"Not so great." Alar spat. "My brother killed himself three weeks ago."

"Oh my God," Zach managed. "I . . . My . . ."

"I know," Alar said. "I heard your Squeal when you started scribing. That's why I talked to you." At this point he spun around again, leaned against the still-beeping car and dry heaved forcefully. He stood there retching and gagging for another couple of minutes. Zach moved forward and put his hand on the small of Alar's back. When he turned around into a half embrace, Zach could see that Alar had burst a blood vessel in his left eye, a starburst of bright red beside the sky blue of iris.

"Hanged himself with an extension cord in his garage," Alar said. "His wife found him."

"I'm so sorry."

"She's a bitch," Alar said, "but I wouldn't wish that on anybody."

They looked at each other for a second.

"Anyway," Zach said. Each of them sort of shrugged. Alar turned away and stumbled sideways into another parked car. Zach cringed.

"Hey, are you going to be alright?"

"I don't know," Alar said. "I'm fucked up." He ran his hands through his hair, spat again. He swayed and his eyes half-closed and rolled back in his head before opening again and focusing on Zach. "Look, I know it's a lot to ask, but would you mind walking me home? I'm just not sure I can make it. I live right around the corner."

"Yeah," Zach said. "I guess I can do that."

THEY STUMBLED ALONG Queen Street, arms around each other's shoulders. There was nothing erotic about their touch now—Alar was barely conscious; every few seconds he'd forget to take a step and he'd end up on his toes, Zach literally dragging him along. Alar's head lolled, and Zach had to keep pinching his side and jabbing into his shoulder with his fingernails to keep him up and get directions. They turned left at Jameson and headed south.

"Alar," Zach said. "Alar! Where next?"

"It's 48 Leopold. Next right."

"Motherfucker." Leopold had been Dan's street the first two years they were dating, before they moved in together. Zach hadn't been on that street since Dan died.

His heart started thudding when they made the turn, shuffled past the piles of garbage and cast-out furniture by the apartment buildings on the corner. He started drawing in big gulps of air, hissing them in through his teeth, blowing them out like a pregnant woman in a Lamaze class. Alar was so out of it he didn't seem to notice. Zach could see the house already, porch lights on, could see the bay windows. He and Dan had sat on the other side of that glass so many nights together, watching TV, cuddling, Dan reading to him from some novel or other. There were different curtains now, he could see as they got closer, some garish floral pattern. Zach's mind was a swirl of memory and emotion, but his legs kept going, one step after the other, dragging and supporting a drunk stranger. He wondered what Dan would think if he could see this.

A moment later, they were past the house, almost before Zach realized it. He craned his head back on his neck to get another glimpse. In his view, the house bobbed with the uneven, imbalanced steps the two of them were taking. It got smaller with every one. Zach turned his head back around and started looking at the numbers on the houses. Within a few more steps, they were at number 48.

Alar came to long enough to say, "It's the main floor," and scrabble around in his pocket for his keys. "Can you do this? The silver one."

Zach leaned Alar against the door frame and opened the door. He wasn't sure what to do. He couldn't imagine walking into the home of some guy he'd just met, after the night he'd just had. But if he left, Alar might still be in trouble.

"Thank you so much," Alar slurred. "Can you put me in my bed? The position where if I barf again in my sleep I won't choke and die?"

Zach chuckled in spite of himself. "Yeah, man. I can do that."

"If you don't hate me, you can crash on my couch. I'll buy you brunch in the morning. You know, to thank you for saving me. We can talk about the pleasures of life after suicide."

"Maybe," Zach said, weaving his arm under Alar's armpits to help him into the house. "No promises."

CAMPING AT
DEAD MAN'S POINT

Certain things about our camping trip never change. It's always the third week of August. It's always men-only. We always meet at the Sobeys at the intersection of Highways 11 and 60 to get groceries before we pick up our gear at Algonquin Outfitters. I was driving up solo, my brother Thomas was driving up with our friend Ron, and Andy was taking his truck and bringing Lewis and Barry. Or so I thought.

When Andy's beat-up Ford pulled into the parking lot, I couldn't help but smile: Dunhill cigarette hanging out of his mouth, bright orange hunting toque on his head, and Bon Jovi blaring out the open windows. Then Lewis got out. I hadn't seen him since last year's trip, and he'd lost a lot of weight. Then some other guy got out of the truck, pale and kind of strange looking.

"Hey, buddy," Andy said, and clapped me in a bear hug.

"Hey, bud," I said. "Who'd you bring?"

"Oh, a guy from my site. Barry couldn't make it—he forgot he had to do some work for his parents this weekend. They wouldn't let him out of it. This is Jim, but we all call him Maury."

I shook his hand—it felt clammy and cold. There was something a little off about Jim, but I couldn't figure out what it was. Lewis started introducing him to the other guys as they headed towards the store. I hung back with Andy, who was finishing his smoke.

"How long have you known him?" I asked.

"A while. He's great. And he's, you know..." Andy waggled his eyebrows at me.

"What?" I asked. Was Andy trying to set us up?

"He's dead."

I guess I had a funny look on my face without realizing it because Andy went on, "Be cool, man—we're all down with your gay shit. Trust me, it's not even that weird."

BUT IT WAS weird. It was weirder than the year Thomas became the only married guy, and got offended by the way the other guys were joking about his wife. It was weirder than the year I came out around the campfire: that silence, all those awkward glances the next day, me trying to convince them all—and myself—that I was still just one of the guys. But this, this... dead guy? It was pretty much the weirdest thing I'd ever seen. I mean, come on: the guy was dead. I don't care how politically incorrect it sounds; I still think it's freakish.

But I tried to put on my roll-with-it face. Guys don't fight during boys' weekend. But Andy knew me too well.

"Sorry I didn't call first," Andy said. "But Barry cancelled last minute, and I didn't want somebody to have to kneel in the middle of one of the canoes—that's so gay. Oops, sorry buddy."

"Suck it," I said. "No, it's cool. Whatever. Always happy to initiate a new guy into the fold! He'll have the time of his life—oops, sorry."

He laughed. "It'll be great—he doesn't even *eat*," Andy emphasized, as though it was the best thing ever. "More food for us!"

WE WALKED AROUND putting stuff in the cart. Andy wanted a double-sized meal of beans and wieners, to get the farts going on the first night. We all basically agreed with that. Then we started discussing which meat to bring and how long it could keep, and the convenience of canned foods versus their weight in the barrel, plus all the other arguments we had every single year. I wandered over to Thomas to talk bro-to-bro.

"Hey, you heard about the new guy?"

"That he's dead? Yeah, no biggie. We have a dead lady at the studio."

I let that settle for a second; I hadn't known. "Do you think the dead guy farts?"

"No, Ron already asked him. He basically has no metabolism—so, no eating, no farting, no puking, nothing. When he died, he only had enough juice left in his balls for a couple more spurts—he froze that, and he's saving it in case he ever meets someone and wants to have kids."

"Are you kidding me?"

"Nope. Welcome to the twenty-first century."

WE PULLED INTO Algonquin Outfitters to pick up our gear—the backpacks, the food barrel, the canoes, paddles, and life jackets, the stove and fuel and pots and pans, waterproof matches. Andy was always pushing for us to buy our own stuff; I fought for renting since I pretty much had it down to a science. The dead guy kind of just hung around the parking lot and smoked. He didn't even offer to help lash the canoes to the roofs of the cars.

Camping at Dead Man's Point

After we pulled into the national park and found spaces beside each other in the gravel lot, Ron and Lewis started unloading stuff and bringing it down to the beach while Andy and I went to get the permits and check in. The girl at the desk looked about seventeen, blond with freckles, and I could tell Andy was into her right away.

She had her feet up on the counter and her nose in a book.

"What are you reading?" Andy asked, as I passed her my driver's licence and the permit application form I'd downloaded and printed.

She tilted the book towards us without looking up.

"*The Id Kid*," Andy read aloud. "Poetry, huh? Cool." I tried not to smirk—Andy never read anything, let alone poetry.

"It's awesome. I want to be a poet after I finish high school."

I tried not to groan—a poet after high school? Who was she, Jewel? Worse, I knew the poet—Linda Besner—and Andy had met her a bunch of times. I was sure he would parlay this into an attempt to pick up the girl, but I was betting on the fact he wouldn't recognize Linda's last name or remember she was a writer. And I certainly wasn't going to help him out. I really just wanted to get out on the water.

In the end, it was the girl who put two and two together. "Matthew J. Trafford," she said, handing me our permit. "I just read a poem about you! You're the one who wrote GAY backwards on his own forehead."

"Yup, that's me," I said. "With eyeliner. I was drunk." This girl just kept staring at me, not even blinking. I gave in. "You know, Linda's a friend of mine. I'll let her know you like her work. Good luck with the writing." I dug a knuckle into Andy's back to signal it was time to leave. If he felt it at all, he didn't let on.

"Yeah, Matthew's my gay friend," Andy said. "But I'm straight." He paused, for way too long. I could feel my cheeks starting to burn. "We're having our annual boys' trip. We have a dead guy with us, too." Was he trying to show her how progressive he was?

"Cool," she said. "Dead people rock."

"I'm going to go help the rest of the guys," I said. "Thanks for this." I waved the permit at the girl. Andy motioned that he'd join me in a minute. I mouthed "She's a child" as I left, but Andy ignored me.

I MET UP with the other guys and we started dividing the gear between the three canoes. Thomas and Ron always paddled together, and Lewis said he'd called paddling with Andy back in the truck, when Jim called shotgun. Which meant I was going to be stuck in the canoe with the dead guy.

Andy finally came out of the office, smiling from ear to ear.

"She said the lake we're going to is totally awesome," he said. We picked a new part of the park every year.

"Baller," Ron said.

"Ball 'er? I fucking wanted to, man. You should have seen her tits. Matthew, even as a gay man, don't you admit they were awesome?"

I pretended not to hear him. What was I supposed to say?

"I should have asked her to come with us. Hey, she said there are these cool campsites at Dead Man's Point that all have access to this amazing cliff for jumping off. If we hurry, maybe we can get one."

"We're only waiting for you," said Lewis pointedly. He clapped Andy on the back. "If you're done flirting, let's go."

Camping at Dead Man's Point

WE ALL GOT our boats into the water, and for twenty minutes we just paddled hard, the wind rushing up into our faces, working our bodies—it felt good. It was what these trips to Algonquin were supposed to be about.

"Which way do we go?" Lewis asked.

"Straight across," Thomas said.

"Gaily forward," I countered. They looked at me. "I don't like to use the word 'straight' in directions. It implies that 'straight' is the only correct path. I don't promote that way of thinking."

Thomas rolled his eyes. I thought I heard the dead man scoff, but it was hard to tell from the back of the canoe. Ron lit a spliff.

"Whatever, man," Andy said. "Isn't there a sleep-away camp for teenage girls on this lake?"

"Yup."

"Let's stay closer to shore and go by it. I want to see some more titties before I go into the wilderness with you faggots. No offence, Matthew."

"Suck my dick," I said.

THERE WAS A little bit of water in the bottom of our canoe and before long it really stank. Sitting in the stern (the dead guy couldn't even steer), I could see it—the water would wash across his feet and little white and grey flakes would come off, and then swish around in the puddle. The sun was beating down on us pretty much directly. The stench was horrible.

"Can you do anything about your, um, foot odour?" I asked.

"That's just the decomp," he said.

"Excuse me?"

"Decomposition," he clarified. As if I'd never seen an epi-sode of *csi*.

"I know what decomp is. I meant: isn't there anything you can do about it?"

"Nope. Comes with the territory. Death ain't pretty. Don't worry, you'll get used to it after a while. I did."

I wanted to point out to him that not breathing had prob-ably been a major factor in that accomplishment, but I didn't want to be too much of a dick. I mean, the guy's feet were flaking off, after all, and he wasn't getting them back.

WHEN WE passed the girls' camp, no one was out swimming. There was just a lifeguard sitting up in one of those tall chairs, wearing a hoodie. We waved at her. She didn't wave back.

"I wonder if she's a squirter," Andy said.

"Quiet," I said. "Sound carries more over the water."

"Who cares?" Then he yelled, "Squirt! Squirt! Squirt!"

This launched all of them into hysterical laughing—I'm not sure why. Eventually I got the giggles, too—there was nowhere for me to hide, and if you can't beat 'em, join 'em, right? It's not like the lifeguard girl even reacted. For the rest of the paddle to the portage, we sang every song we could think of, changing almost all of the words to "squirt."

THE LAKE NARROWED as we approached the portage, and we could see several canoes coming up behind us.

"OK, guys," Ron said, "we have to do this portage in one trip. We have to beat these assholes so we can get to the campsites with the cliff. Let's get 'er done!"

"Git 'er done!" we all yelled.

We totally creamed those other guys on the portage. Even the dead guy kept up. Ron, Andy, and Lewis took a canoe

Camping at Dead Man's Point

each, and the rest of us doubled up on packs and gear. All in all, we were making pretty good time, feeling good about ourselves. Then as we got back in the water and rounded a little bend, drifting through the marshy grasses, we saw a canoe coming the other way. It was clearly a father-son combo—the dad looked like an old hippie type and the son looked nerdy and weird.

"Looks like you guys got a late start!" the man said. None of us really said anything back, just kind of waved and smiled.

When we were safely out of earshot, we let it rip.

"Looks like *you* got a late start, asshole."

"I know, as if! It's only four o'clock, this lake is tiny, and we still have at least four or five hours of daylight!"

"What a dick turd."

"I should have told him it was because I'm the *late* Jim Lundy," the dead guy said. Ron was nice enough to groan at the pun. "That's actually how my mail is addressed now, you know. The Late Jim Lundy. Or sometimes just to my estate."

"So are you allowed to, like, own property and shit?"

"My estate is. It's basically the same thing, it's just not as attached to me directly. More free."

"Cool."

"I don't get to vote though."

"Oh, I never vote," Ron exhaled. "Who cares?"

"Let's get going," Lewis said. "What's the holdup?"

"I'm still thinking about that office girl's tits," Andy said.

THE NEXT HOUR of the trip pretty much sucked, even though it only took us ten minutes to get to the campsite with the cliff—way less than we expected. We approached

from the cliff side, saw it looming above us, the rock slick
and wet, mosses and lichens growing on its face.

"Fuck man, this is wicked," Andy said. "That's got to be
thirty feet high!"

"Geronimo!" someone yelled, and then a fit twenty-
something in a tight boykini cannonballed into the water
beside us.

"Jesus, that's dangerous," Lewis said. "He could've landed
right on top of us."

"Worse, it means at least one of the campsites is already
gone," I said. Mr. Reality.

The twenty-something's head came up out of the water,
flashing perfect teeth at us. He looked like he was barely
starting his twenties, whereas the rest of us were practically
thirty, and it showed.

"Hey guys," he said, whipping his bangs back in a wet
pompadour.

"What were you thinking?" Lewis asked. "That was total
danger bay! You could have landed right on us."

"I was nowhere near you," the twenty-something said. He
made eye contact with me and kind of smiled, then looked
around at all the other guys, trying to figure us out. I noticed
him lingering over Jim. "Plus, I didn't expect anyone to still
be on the water this late in the afternoon. You guys got a late
start, huh?"

"Fuck off," muttered Lewis.

"Guess so," Ron said. "So you're camping here at the cliff?"

"Yup," he said, treading water. "It's our Fairies and Bears
weekend."

"What?" asked Lewis.

"Gay guys," Thomas explained. "Fairies. Bears are gay
guys who are fat and hairy."

Camping at Dead Man's Point

"A bunch of queers gone camping?" This from the dead guy. The swimmer looked at me quizzically, still treading. He seemed relaxed, like he could do it for hours without getting tired.

"Yes, Jim," I said dryly. "Queers camp, too. What do you think I'm doing?" I turned back to the guy. "Are there any other sites free?"

"Sorry, dudes. There're five sites here at Dead Man's Point, and they're all taken. Last group came in two hours ago. You might have better luck across the way."

We all grumbled. "Thanks anyway," I said.

"Listen." He ducked his head under the water, flipping his hair back again when he came up. "We're having a big barbeque and party tomorrow night. We've got tonnes of food and booze. Depending where you guys end up, you should paddle on over. Everyone's welcome to come."

"I bet they are," Andy said. "Get us to pass out drunk and then we wake up with half a pack of Trojans up our asses."

"Jesus, Andy," I mumbled. It was all I could muster.

"Nice friends you've got there," the swimmer said, looking me in the eyes. "See ya."

NO ONE SAID anything as he swam back to the shore. I was staring at the muscles of his back, until I noticed the other two canoes had already turned around. I manoeuvred us between them, feeling something funny in my stomach. We weren't going to get the site we wanted, because a bunch of fairies and bears had beaten us to the punch. I was embarrassed by them, and felt responsible somehow. I thought we could use a joke to lighten up the mood.

"Hey, Jim," I said. "You should go up there and scare the shit out of them."

"What?"

"Like, say that you're the dead man the point is named after, and that you want them off your land, and do a bunch of zombie shit to freak them out."

"I'm not a fucking zombie, OK? Jesus."

"You're a dead guy who walks around, isn't that a zombie?"

"No, you gay asshole. Zombies are stupid, and eat brains— you seen me eating any brains?"

"Easy buddy. God, I'm sorry. I haven't seen you eating any brains."

"You think I'm stupid?"

"No, I don't think you're stupid. Jim, it was just a joke..."

"It wasn't funny," he said. "I'm not mixed up in voodoo and horror movies and shit like that. I'm just dead. Just a normal guy from Halton County, but I'm dead. And you will be, too, one day."

"Thanks for the reminder," I managed. Why wasn't anyone else getting my back? Changing the subject at least?

"No problem," Jim said. "That's why they call me Maury."

"What do you mean?"

"*Memento mori*—it's Latin for 'remember you will die.'"

"That's creepy, dude. We came here to relax, not contemplate mortality."

"Call it what you want. Death gives life meaning. I'm a reminder of that, too."

"It's hard to believe my life has any meaning at all if I just keep dwelling on the fact I'm going to drop dead at the end of it. Plus, as your being here so clearly points out, death isn't necessarily the end." I kept going, not wanting to let him get a word in. "What the hell are you then, if you're not a zombie? The living dead?"

"Nothing living about me, friend. We prefer the term 'undead.' 'Undead' will do just fine."

"How was I supposed to know? Sorry man."

Camping at Dead Man's Point

"Ignorance is no excuse."

"You really want to get into a conversation with me about *ignorance* right now?"

Thomas ended it. "If you girls are done, we need to find somewhere to camp for tonight. Come on, let's get moving."

WE PADDLED IN silence for a while, which made me feel even worse. I didn't want to pick a fight with the guy and ruin the vibe for everyone, but at the same time there was something about Jim I just couldn't stand. I tried to start another round of squirt songs to lighten the mood, but it didn't really work. We ended up at what would have been a totally awesome site if we weren't comparing it to the cliff-jumping haven across the bay.

We kind of naturally divided up into teams—two guys set up the tents, two started on the fire, and two collected wood. Andy was on wood, since he'd brought an axe and a machete (not to mention a slingshot with surgical tubing and a pound of buckshot, which looked to me like a bunch of ball bearings). He took Jim with him, which I appreciated, and the mood of the group palpably relaxed. Ron and I were working on the tents.

"Hey, sorry if I lost my shit back there," I said.

"Don't worry about it, man. He was being really sensitive. I would have called him a zombie, too—I didn't know that was offensive. Shit."

"Right? I've never hung out with a dead guy before."

"Me neither. He seems cool enough though. He seems like a good guy."

"Yeah, totally. We just got off on the wrong foot."

"Yup."

"Speaking of which, did you smell his? Feet, I mean."

"No, were they bad?"

"Holy shit man—I was practically gagging in the canoe. Those things fucking reek."

"Guess you don't want to share a tent with him, then?"

"Fuck no. Let's give him to Andy. He brought him."

"No argument here, man."

THINGS ACTUALLY GOT better after that. The beans and wieners were delicious, just what we wanted after a long day. We were too lazy to make s'mores, so we just ate the ingredients raw out of the boxes and packets. We sparked a couple doobies and passed them around, and we'd been drinking whisky since we arrived at the site. Jim wasn't eating or drinking, of course, but you didn't really notice in the dark. We were just men, sitting around a fire, passing a bottle and eating hot food, and it was good. We shot the shit, talked about nothing in particular, and looked up at the stars in the silent moments.

"Hey, what about Elvis?" Ron asked.

No one said anything for a minute.

"What about him?" Lewis finally asked.

"Well like, did he really die, or is he still alive? Or is he like, undead, and that's why people think they see him? I just thought maybe Jim would know."

We all looked at Jim.

"I don't fucking know," he said. "It's not like we get a list. We don't have meetings."

"Don't let them rile you," I said. "They asked me a lot of stupid gay questions when I first came out. Like whether or not it was true about Tom Cruise."

"I don't know anything about that shit," Jim said. "And I don't want to, either."

Camping at Dead Man's Point

I shrugged that off.

Andy got up at one point to add some more wood, and the pieces he put on had needles on them that caught fire in a noisy sputter and jumped and swirled in the air. The wood was dry and cracked a lot, and orange sparks would shoot up into the dark like fireworks, landing on our pants and feet and forearms, leaving little burn marks. Jim got up and shuffled the stump he was sitting on a few feet back.

"The fire freaks me out," he said.

"You ever been burned?" Thomas asked. "I knew a girl whose nightie caught fire from an electric heater when she was eight, and she was afraid of fire, even matches, for the rest of her life."

"No, nothing like that," Jim said.

"Remember that girl in elementary school," I said, turning to Thomas, "who was playing with a candle on Sunday morning, and when her parents came to call her for church, she thought it would be a good idea to hide the thing under the couch, still lit? Burned the whole bloody house down while they were out!"

We all laughed our asses off. It was quiet for a minute.

"No," Jim said. "It's just that, if I get burnt, or catch fire, that's it for me, you know? Not that catching fire is a picnic for anyone, but there's no coming back from that for me. I can't regenerate, right? No skin grafts for me anymore."

We were quiet, thinking it over. Lewis shuffled his feet a bit.

"You guys don't realize how amazing your bodies are. You take them for granted, drinking like that and smoking that shit, eating such crappy food."

"Whoa," Ron said. "Easy."

"Your bodies are temples, men. The things your cells can do? They're constantly replacing themselves, making perfect copies. Your hair is growing, all the time! Your fingernails. You cut yourself, and your blood clots and your skin heals together, and makes a scar—that's incredible! It's a miracle! Shit, I'd kill for that."

It was a poor choice of words. We were all suddenly a little afraid that he was going to do something to us in our sleep. Steal our bodies, somehow. I think he sensed that he'd gone a little too far.

"I guess I'll turn in now," he said. "Not that I actually need to sleep."

He shuffled off towards the tents, found the one he and Andy were sharing, and unzipped the flap and went in.

"Man," Ron said, his voice low, "that dude is a little creepy."

"Aw, don't worry guys, he's fine," Andy said. "Sometimes he just gets a little maudlin about being dead, that's all. He's harmless."

"What about bears?" Lewis slurred.

"No worries," Thomas said. "We already hung the food barrel in that tree. It's cool."

"No, I mean because of Jim. Won't they smell him? Isn't he basically, like, meat?"

Thomas started giggling, which made me start giggling, too.

"Shhh!" Andy tried to hush us.

"I don't want to be rude," Ron said, "but he kind of has a point."

"I guess . . . but, like, he's no more meat than we are, right?"

"I don't know, man," Lewis said. "But we have, like, pheromones and shit, and fucking *breathing*, and pulses, and the bears can smell us and hear us and know we're, like, *alive*, and so they're cautious around us and stuff. But he's just a dead body—don't bears eat the dead?"

Camping at Dead Man's Point

"No. They don't. Well, I don't know. Do they?"

"Aren't they, like, omnivores?"

"I don't know! You want to bring it up with him? I'm sure it's fine."

"It better be." Lewis took another swig of the whisky. "I'm not getting mauled just because you brought some dead fucker with us."

"It's cool, man," Andy said. "Just go to bed."

"Hey," a voice came from the tents. "Are you guys talking about me?"

"No, man," Andy said.

"No way!"

"OK then."

"We're all coming to bed soon," I said. And as soon as I said it, there was nothing else to do but head up to the tents.

ONE OTHER THING that never changes about the camping trip is the Second Day Debate. It doesn't always happen on the second day, but this time it did. The debate is whether to stay at the site we're at, and just relax, or pack up all our stuff and paddle around, hoping there's another free site on one of the lakes we have a permit for. The debate didn't take long this year—we were all hungover, and we knew from the day before that the whole lake was pretty full. The only problem with staying put and relaxing was that some guys got bored.

Andy decided to chill out on a rock with his feet in the water and play with his slingshot. Mostly he was aiming at a submerged stump a few feet away, until Lewis pointed out a loon that surfaced nearby with two adolescents, who weren't quite black and didn't yet have spots.

"Hey Andy, look!" he said. "Fresh meat."

Andy took aim at the loon and her children with the slingshot.

"Andy!" I was shocked.

"What?" he said. "It's awesome, man."

"You can't do that!" I said. "That's horrible. This is a national park! It's to *protect* wildlife."

"Oh, lighten up," Lewis said.

"Yeah," said Andy. "Don't be so gay." That pissed me off—he hadn't said it like it was a joke. He drew back on the slingshot and released it, and the ball bearing splashed ridiculously close to the loons.

"Good one!" Lewis called out, laughing.

I was stuck. Whenever the guys ganged up on me, played the gay card, I felt like there was nothing I could do. Anything I said would only make it worse, give them more fodder to use to make fun of me. I wanted to walk away, but I was too worried about the birds.

Jim looked up from his magazine. "Andy! Don't be such a dick. How old are you, anyway? That bird's a living creature. Have some fucking respect."

Andy and Lewis looked at each other. The bird dove, followed by its kids.

"Whatever," Andy said. "It's gone now, anyway."

Jim caught my eye before returning to whatever he was reading. I thought he smiled a bit, but I couldn't really see. Maybe things were going to be OK between us.

THROUGHOUT THE DAY we would see canoes with other groups of people on the lake, looking for campsites that weren't occupied yet, or returning from more remote lakes to the access point we had started at. If they were women, the guys made jokes about fucking them. If they were men,

Camping at Dead Man's Point

I kept my mouth shut—the year before I'd made some comments about a couple of hot shirtless guys paddling by, and it hadn't gone over well. As the afternoon wore on, the comments got more and more taboo—part of being free and wild, out of the city—and somehow or other they turned to murder.

"Hey, let's go kill those people later."

"Totally, raiding party, like old-school pirates or Vikings or something."

"No, like Indians, dumb-ass. Duh."

"I'm going to take my axe and kill them all."

"I'll use the slingshot."

The dead guy didn't say anything. I wasn't surprised, after the way he'd been about the loon. I wanted to say something, but kept my mouth shut as usual—and the guys were totally oblivious to his body language and mood. They were getting really vicious with it, trying to outdo each other and gross each other out.

"I'm going to cut off their heads," Lewis said, "and eat my dinner out of their skulls like a cannibal."

"Too far!" Ron groaned.

I was still watching Jim's face. He looked unhappy and far away. Suddenly it came to me.

"Hey man, how'd you die, anyway?" I asked him. I said it loud enough so everyone could hear me.

"I was murdered, actually," he said. He looked down when he said it.

"Oh, shit, sorry dude." I felt sick to my stomach.

"Yeah, sorry man."

"Sorry Jim."

"Sorry Maury. Hey, that rhymes."

"Jesus Andy, have a heart. And why didn't you tell us? Sorry Jim."

"Didn't know," Andy said. "I guess we never asked."

"It's OK," Jim said. "Living people just don't think about it." He scratched his head. I saw that some of his hair stuck under his fingernails and came out when he brought his hand back down. "It was a home invasion, and it was over fast. Look, I know you guys were just joking about killing those people, obviously. But it's not funny when it, you know, has actually happened to you."

He headed off towards the woods. I looked at Andy, and he made a 'let him go' kind of motion with his hand. But I decided to follow him.

"Hey Jim, wait up," I called. He looked surprised. "I just wanted to apologize again," I said. "I know what it's like. Those guys make fag jokes all the time, call things they don't like 'gay.' I know they don't mean it to be offensive, but it still hurts; it's still not right."

"Oh come on," Jim said.

"What?"

"Don't compare us. That's not the same thing at all. You don't know the first thing about what it's like to be me."

"I'm not saying I do, Jim. But... we're both invisible minorities, right? Trying to fit in to a world that doesn't necessarily get us... we're not so different."

"It's night and day, Matthew. I know I'm the new one here, so I've been biting my tongue, but I don't care for gays at all. All those queers flaunting it across the bay in those tiny swim shorts, looking at your prissy face all day. Andy didn't tell me there'd be a fag on the trip—I wouldn't have come."

"Hey, let's not get out of hand," I said. I started panicking, but instead of shutting up I kept running my mouth, trying to reason with him. "There are probably just things about it you don't understand, like how we're still learning about undead people."

"I told you it's not the same," he said. "I think homosexuality is disgusting and unnatural."

"Unnatural?" I raised my voice. "You're a fucking corpse! You're supposed to be dead!"

"I'm *un*dead!" he shouted back. He turned away and headed into the woods, and I went back to the guys.

"What'd he say?" Ron asked.

"Nothing," I said. I grabbed the axe and started hacking away at a log, hard as I could. "I shouldn't have followed him."

JIM CAME BACK about an hour later, in a good mood and acting like nothing had happened. He and Thomas went for a paddle around the bay, then he and Lewis played Frisbee for a while. I was pretty sure he was giving me the silent treatment, but it wasn't in a way the other guys would notice. I decided to just let it ride. No need to make things worse. I could keep my cool.

We started drinking way before it got dark. We could hear the sounds of the fairies and bears party across the bay—I didn't even bother to suggest going over, even though I was curious about it, given what had happened with Jim. Instead I hit the sauce hard. I was mad, despite myself, and pissed off that I had to cut a wide conversational berth around someone who wasn't even supposed to be part of the trip. Dead or undead or whatever he was, why was I letting his bullshit exclude me from hanging out with my friends? It was just stupid.

I was trying to let it go, but he bothered me. For some reason I kept thinking about what Thomas had said about the dead guy maybe wanting to artificially inseminate someone in the future. That sounded pretty "unnatural" to me. And if he couldn't get women pregnant the usual way, did he even have sex? *Could* he have sex, physically?

"Hey, Jim, you get boners?"

"Hardest stiffy you ever saw on a stiff!"

I was really getting sick of all his dead puns. "But if your heart's not beating, how do you get the blood in there?"

"I inject myself with an anticoagulant to keep my blood liquid, and then I sort of have to force it into my dick. I have a pump."

"Sounds complicated."

"Well, at least I don't fuck guys up the ass."

Andy and Thomas laughed. Lewis made a hissing noise and held up his hands like claws. "Cat fight!" he said.

"I'm going to the kybo," I said.

"Don't fall in," said the dead guy. I couldn't think of a comeback to that.

IT WAS MY turn to sulk in the woods for a bit—I figured twenty minutes was the longest I could go without them realizing I was doing more than relieving myself. When I got back, they had the fire going and were cooking. Thomas called me over to a spot near where he was sitting and handed me a plate of meat that was so charred on the outside I couldn't recognize what it was. But it was delicious anyway. The whisky was almost gone and someone had opened a big bottle of wine.

They were talking about Tom Thomson. He had died in the park, and apparently there was a memorial monument to him on the first lake that none of us had bothered to notice.

"Who's Tom Thomson?" Lewis asked.

Camping at Dead Man's Point

"A famous painter." Thomas said. "He was friends with all the guys from the Group of Seven. But before they formed he got drunk and went out in his canoe and drowned."

"I thought they didn't know for sure what happened," I said. Thomas shrugged.

"God, I wonder how many people have died out here," Ron said. I was starting to get uncomfortable again. Couldn't we go five minutes without talking about death?

"A bunch," Andy said.

"You have no idea what it's like," Jim said. "To die. I hope you don't have to know for a long time. And I hope you get to know what it is to be undead, too. There's nothing like it."

"How does one get to be undead, anyway?" I asked, turning to Jim. "I've never really understood that."

"It's a very private process, actually," Jim said. "It's something you have to work out on the other side, before you come back. It's difficult to explain to the living."

"But you just brought it up."

"Hey, lay off him. Lay off." This was Andy.

I wasn't in the mood. I was sick of laying off. "But it's something you *choose*, right? It's not just something you're born with, like being gay?"

"Matthew, don't get political," Thomas said.

"No, I just want to know. Maybe Jim can enlighten us. He seems to love to hear himself talk."

"You're drunk," Lewis said. I glared at him. "And I love it," he added.

"Being undead is a privilege, not a right. It's just another way of understanding the transition. Death doesn't have to be the end."

"I don't buy any of that shit. That's what bothers me with you undead people—you don't take anything seriously, not even death! You die and you just keep on going like nothing important has happened!"

"Hey now, come on," Andy said. But Jim and I were in our own zone now, not listening to anybody else.

"Well, to me, whether my body is alive or dead just isn't how I define who and what I am. I don't place the same importance on death that the mainstream culture does."

"You're fucking dead!"

"I don't see why that matters to you so much. Maybe you're dead," he pointed at me. "On the inside."

"Oh fuck you, Jim," I said. "And fuck your *memento mori*."

"Matthew, man," Lewis said, "just sit down. You're getting hysterical."

"Don't call me that. Why are you siding with the corpse? He's a homophobe and he's full of shit. And you know what? You never would have used that word on any of the other guys. You're calling me hysterical just because I'm gay."

"I'm calling you hysterical because you're screaming like a woman and not making any sense. Now sit down, calm the fuck down, and leave Jim alone."

I looked at my friends, who I'd been coming up here with for years. They were staring at me like I was crazy. In the firelight, I couldn't recognize their faces.

"You know what? Fuck all of you."

I STORMED OFF to the beach and set out in one of the canoes, ridiculously drunk. I kept thinking: this is how Tom Thomson died; this is how Tom Thomson died. But I didn't care. I had to get out of there, away from the dead guy, away from all of those guys. I steered the canoe towards the cliff site, Dead Man's Point. I wasn't sure what I was going to do when

Camping at Dead Man's Point

I got there, *if* I got there, empty-handed and already drunk. Probably I would look for the guy from the cliff, apologize for my asshole friends, and ask if I could still join in with them. They'd be nice to me; tell me which ones of them were single and try to set me up, or maybe we'd just hang out in a big group, a bunch of gays, and we'd have an orgy by the light of the fire, just like in a porn. Or else they'd simply welcome me, a lost and weary traveller, and when I told them why I was there, they would agree with me that being dead was just too damn weird.

VICTIM SERVICES

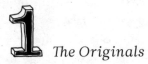 *The Originals*

NELITH & KIYOMA

Nelith and Kiyoma coming to Canada, immigrants landed, English learned, queuing at consulates and securing citizenship, combatting the frigid climate and foreign customs to create a new home, seeking solace and opportunity in a colony turned country whose independence hadn't cascaded into cultures killing each other like the Sinhalese and Tamils did back home. Nelith beaming when their baby was born a boy, a Canadian child safe from frequent floods and fighting; naming him Sumen. Nelith and Kiyoma scouting schools, exuberant, not knowing the improbable consequence of their choice, that Canada cheated, showboating wealth and safety but selecting a psychopath to practice pedagogy. Kiyoma keening at the death of the child she'd created and cared for, her Sumen, killed callously and catastrophically, killed in the classroom. Nelith and Kiyoma regretting and rueful, bitter and broken, betrayed.

MICHAEL

Michael sitting topless on the end of his bed, listening to his mothers argue about something he doesn't understand, impatient to get dressed and start his new adventure, *going to school*, excited to meet other kids who would be there every day, to not have to rely on the random chance of nice weather and Mama saying yes to the park and getting there when other boys were there for him to play with, hopefully with a ball for catch or soccer. He was excited too for snacks and listening to stories and learning to be smart like grownups are—Mama and Mommy had told him what a fun place it would be. Michael seeing his Velcro sneakers on the floor nearby, knowing he could get those on and fastened all by himself, waiting for his Mama to finally select a t-shirt and put it on him and get him out of his house and into the car seat and to the school and inside the classroom where he belonged. Mommy was talking to Mama in the quiet-dry voice she used when something was wrong, saying words like "bullying" and "outcast" that Michael didn't understand, like he didn't understand why he couldn't wear his *2 PROUD MOMMIES* t-shirt to school, like he didn't understand why it was taking so long to just pick something else and put it on and get there. Michael putting his pyjama top back on to try to help out, his mothers seeing this, Mama laughing, Mommy pretending not to, finally choosing a plain blue shirt. Michael putting his arms up as the shirt came down over his hands and head, Michael running down to the car, Michael jumping out of it, running to join the kids in the yard at school without once looking back.

DANIEL & JOANNE

Joanne working on the note at home, late at night; Joanne bringing it to school but too afraid to pass it; Joanne crying at lunch break about the note and being too scared to give it to Carla; Carla taking the note from Joanne and promising she would *deal with it* and deliver it, unopened. Carla passing the note to Caroline and whispering in the middle of math class, while Miss Maple wrote numerators and lowest common denominators on the blackboard; Caroline passing it to Noreen, a smile at her lips; Noreen passing it to Paula, eyes boring the importance of it into Paula's timid face; Paula poking Sumen with her pencil three times before he finally turned around and looked at her; Sumen feeling funny as he passed the note to Daniel: "Here Dan, it's for you."

Daniel reading the note half inside his desk, as he'd practised with comic books, Miss Maple having caught him only twice this entire school year. Daniel memorizing the note's simple message and instructions. Daniel rushing to the art shelf when the bell rang for recess, running his ink-smeared hands over the bottles of glue, selecting one, literally swiping it off the shelf and letting it drop into one deep pocket of his jeans, which rode well below his hips. Daniel shuffling to the meeting place as set out in the note: the kindergarten sandbox, where they hadn't played in years.

Joanne waiting, her crutches lying on the ground beside her, a long clear tube of gold glitter in her hand. Joanne saying, "I swiped mine. Did you get yours?" Daniel showing her the bottle of white glue.

Daniel and Joanne, barely realizing their hands are touching, squeezing the glue out in the shape of a heart, a sticky thread upon the cracked wooden frame of the sandbox, sprinkling the gold sparkles all over the heart and the *D + J* inside. Joanne saying, "Now we're going steady." Daniel saying, "It's official—at least until the end of grade three." Joanne saying, "We're going to get married. I just know it."

Daniel and Joanne, six days from their last.

Victim Services

2 *The Victims*

EDMUND & DENISE

Edmund in exile, far away from the life he knew while still appearing to live it; his body foreign to him, waking each day as though shot put balls from his high school track team were strapped to his chest and to each of his limbs; his emotions strange and stormy, deterring him from examining their erratic patterns, or, God forbid, sharing them with his wife, crying each time he passed by Shane's room and saw the *Spiderwick* posters still taped to the closet door, feeling angry all the time without warning or due cause; Edmund cast out from the comforts of carnal union with Denise, not because of headaches or demure excuses or the emotional expanse between them, not because of her at all, but cast out by his own complete lack of interest, a disinterest in sex that he never before would have believed possible; Edmund in exile from the rituals and satisfactions of mealtime, a dearth of appetite not only for the heavy, buttery food Denise prepared but even the offerings of his favourite five-star restaurant, a place he used to go weekly with his male friends; exiled, in short, from an ability to enjoy anything about his life at all, exiled from what was normal by the death of his nine-year-old son.

Edmund estranged in some subtle way from his buoyant wife, his wife whose daily habits suddenly revolted him— the way she brushed her hair in the morning, just for one small example, pulling long coiling hairs out of the brush and dropping them onto the bathroom floor—his wife whose fiery French temper seemed brash for the first time ever, his wife who'd had the audacity to find a way to go on and be happy, somehow happy; his wife who, in her happiness, was being cautious and reluctant about the letter they'd received, the official letter from the Government of Canada, all standard fonts and black-and-white reproductions of the flag and information in both official languages, the letter from the Victim Services department proposing an experimental new project. His wife who at his request dutifully read the guidelines he'd downloaded as a PDF and printed out using their family computer, his wife who laughed at the French translations as though this document were a cereal box or the nutritional info on a bag of potato chips, his wife whose lack of gravitas wounded Edmund, pushed him farther away. His wife who wanted to say *"Non!"*

Edmund, straining to convince her, exhorting her for hours, imploring her to hear, persuading not with well-constructed arguments or reasonable phrases, not with assurances or certainties or earnest promises or proofs, but by using something primal, something stronger, something Shane himself had often used: Edmund pouted, Edmund pleaded, Edmund knelt down on two knees. Edmund whispered softly, "I need this. I need this. I need this."

Edmund reduced to begging.

SHANNON

Shannon scrapbooking, pruning photos and pasting clever captions, decorating each page with Paula's pristine memory. Shannon sifting through craft store shelves, picking kits with buttons, soft strips, Citrus Brad Packs and Petal Pushers, phrase makers and chipboard shapes. Shannon thrilling at the arrival of an envelope: a letter from the Canadian government, screaming "special moment" for her Special Moments Page. Shannon had been searching for something so perfect, something to surround with sparkle and shimmering stickers and a Flowers and Frills Filigree Press-On Accent. So excited was Shannon that she almost forgot to open it, almost glued it in still sealed. But Shannon's artist eye caught the straightness of the line, thought the page looked insincere with the letter sealed shut, so she picked up her pewter letter opener with the pearl-studded unicorn handle, slipped it nimbly into the envelope, and sliced through the paper as if it were air.

Shannon stunned, Shannon disbelieving, Shannon's mouth shaped like a sodden Cheerio in milk. Shannon knowing—almost before her eyes finished flicking across the page—that she would say yes, not just agree to it but say: "Yes! Yes! A million times yes!" Shannon applauding the proposal to bring her daughter back.

Shannon learning the letter, memorizing, repeating its legal terms and convoluted phrases, saying "experimental project proposal from Victim Services" to her reflection in the mirror, enunciating each syllable, saying "regenesis does not mean replacement" as she walked to work each day, saying "your NeoKid™ will not be the child you lost but a perfect genetic match," saying "the baby will not know you," saying "you will have to raise your child again" and getting excited at that notion, saying "think of the NeoKid™ as a twin sibling born years later," impossible to do, photocopying the letter for scrapbook purposes, surrounding pasted copies with Jellishments and epoxy stickers, knowing that despite the warnings she expected no one but her Paula to return.

GORDON & JUNE

Gordon, never before today having stepped inside the school let alone the gymnasium, which smells of sweaty rubber, never having sat in folding chairs, never having dealt with clandestine advisory council meeting politics or the petty complaints of other parents, never so much as having sat silent witness at a parent-teacher interview, believing their daughter's education was June's domain, a place inappropriate for a father who could better spend his time earning money for his family: his wife, June, his daughter, Joanne, and the team of doctors that had worked hard and long to make sure Joanne stayed alive. Gordon apoplectic that his daughter's life was taken after all his work to save her, finding a way to see—and pay—every specialist around, bringing his daughter to her appointments, holding her hand in every waiting room and office, telling her not to be afraid.

Gordon fearing the crescendo of his blood pressure like the onslaught of a train. Gordon getting flushed, popping handfuls of antacids, combatting roiling heartburn. Gordon getting angry, grabbing his ears in frustration, not realizing how odd this looked or even that he'd done it. Gordon getting loud and speaking out of turn, glaring at the parents who opposed what he was for. *Meddling. Playing God.* As if removing a child's disease was a crime against them all. Gordon knew the parents' problem, that they saw a can of worms. They were afraid of those parents who would want everything to change, eye colour and IQ, body type and hair. They lumped them all together, refused the shades of grey, saw one damned *slippery slope* with Gordon at the top.

But Gordon knew persuasion, knew rhetoric, knew bribes, knew the scientists would *have* to try whether or not they should. Gordon got what Gordon wanted, or Gordon didn't play. Gordon watched the scientist raise his hand to shush the gathered crowd of parents, and Gordon heard the words with relief but not surprise: "As for genetic modifications, we're going to go ahead. No one has to change a single thing about their child. But if you want changes, we can do that. Think of Gordon and June, here: a certain percentage of the children they conceive will have Hoffmann-Kuhn disease, and a certain percentage won't. All we're doing here is switching their NeoKid™ over into the group that doesn't."

Gordon grinned and took deep breaths and reached for June's cool hand. This was justice in its most pure form, cosmic justice they'd never dared to hope for. Not only would their new child avoid Miss Maple and her madness, but also be free of the debilitation that had made their first daughter's life so hard. It was a fresh start, a second chance— Gordon getting something he didn't know life had to give.

3 The Crime

MISS MAPLE

The many modes of Miss Maple: Miss Maple, sleek and slender, dressed in sheer blouses and smart slacks, short skirts and Spring Sale discounted pantsuits; Miss Maple excelling at teachers' college, exceeding expectations for student-teacher placement, practicum perfected; Miss Maple securing positions, full-time grade three; Miss Maple, exuding politesse and exacting proper classroom behaviour; Miss Maple, Miss Maple, Miss Maple. Marvellous Maple! Miss Maple the perfectionist, working long hours, bringing doughnuts and coffee to the custodial staff as penance for staying in her room so late, getting in their way and disrupting their rhythm of scraping gum from desks and sweeping floors with giant flop-brooms; Miss Maple laminating early in the morning, coffee in hand and something aloof in her eyes, fixed mid-distance; Miss Maple cutting bulletin-board borders and phonics charts, tangram sets for math lessons

and placemats for lunchtime, flash cards for spelling, gathering materials for arts and crafts, collating popsicle sticks,
Styrofoam cups, and pennies for science lessons on levers
and pulleys, catapults; Miss Maple reading picture books
to rapt and upturned faces; Miss Maple winning teacher of
the year three times in a row. Miss Maple on ladders: step-
ladders to staple laminated borders all around the room, to
stick push pins through brightly painted family portraits
into corkboard; tall ladders for hanging turkeys made from
the cut-out silhouettes of the children's hands in autumn,
carefully rendered snowflakes in winter, always something
delicate and papery dangling from the light fixtures; Miss
Maple on ladders at home, checking the height of the roof
against the resilience of human vertebrae, checking the
sturdiness of ceiling beams against different thicknesses
of rope and her oft-fluctuating body weight. Miss Maple
on bicycles: on her bicycle to and from the school, to and
from environmental rallies and peace marches, to and from
her therapist's office, to and fro, fro and to; Miss Maple in
tears: tears on her pillow, tears in her ears, dripped cold at
night and slow to come, bloodshot tears, hot tears at inappropriate times, rushing into the bathroom tears, midway
through a harmless conversation tears; Miss Maple weeping alone, unseen, in her apartment. Miss Maple marking:
stacks of hand-printed stories stolen from television or the
very picture books she'd read in class; math tests full of dys-
lexic threes and ineptly drawn function signs, sloppy long
division; spelling tests and lab reports and fledgling essays.
Miss Maple repeating the names of her beloved students to
get herself to sleep, counting them like sheep, like lambs:
gentle cowlicked Shane, whose syllables had an adorable
half-accent he'd inherited from his mother, still dropping

h's from the beginning of words, *appy to see you, math is too ard;* the sporty boys Michael and Brian and Hashi and Luco; the nerdy boys Sumen and Daniel, always with comic books and breathless stories of Saturday cartoons shared all throughout each Monday; the girls, Jordana and Carla and Leslie, who already at nine were starting to apply coloured glosses like lipstick, who wore big hoop earrings, who seemed to almost have the buds of breasts; Beth and Caroline who liked sports but were too embarrassed to show it; dark-haired Noreen who didn't care and loved hockey and always got to be goalie; irrepressible Joanne who had overcome crutches and a rare degenerative disease, bright-eyed and trusting; Paula, forever emotional and on the verge of tears herself, who missed a week of school when she'd discovered the tooth fairy wasn't real; all the sweet children Miss Maple loved so much, twenty-eight little angels. She loved them, and she feared for them as well: for what their futures held, STDs and unplanned pregnancies, rushed-into marriages and messy divorces, diseased parents in expensive nursing homes, unrealized dreams; but she was even more afraid for the ever-rising lack of biodiversity, all the species they would never see; the slow economic plunder of Canada, the inevitable exploitation and rape of this country and her softwood lumber, her fresh water; the terrorist attacks they were bound to witness; the miles and miles of coastline that would be underwater by the time they were twenty; the floods of eco-refugees from submerged land masses; the wars over natural resources; in short, all the looming disaster and decimation earned by a species too long on the planet, wrought by these children's parents and grandparents but which only they would suffer, unjustly, undeservedly. And how despite her best efforts and theirs they would make things worse, just by virtue of being North American and used to this level of consumption, just by breathing, and worse still, by procreating, stupidly bringing more and more children into this dying, ridiculous world. And when she'd cycled through these thoughts and their endless variations a million times or more, when she solidified her love and her fear into a plan, an Earth Day lesson, when she had crystallized her reasoning into an articulate handwritten letter, sealed and left in the middle of her desk blotter, after she'd scared the children by pouring boiling water into the class aquarium to simulate global warming, poured in bleach to simulate pollution, after the children had started crying as the fish one by one turned belly-up and floated, when she could look in each of their eyes and feel that they understood, understood her fear and her love and her purpose, that they shared it, that they had in fact become a beautiful collective consciousness, she gave them the treats she had prepared, the special Earth Day snacks, the organic apple cider from the local orchard, and the brownies, smeared with thick icing, thick enough to give Joanne and some of the less chocoholic children pause, before they too gave in and happily chomped the brownies down, everyone stuffing themselves, smiling carob-sweet smiles, all of them, together, including Miss Maple herself.

4 *The NeoKids*™

DOT

Dot not objecting to her listless son and blithe daughter-in-law wanting another child, encouraging them in anything meant to break the atmosphere of gloom that had hung in the house like fog since Shane had died. Dot, like Denise, initially against the idea of cloning the poor boy, disturbing

Victim Services

the dead for a process entirely unnatural. Dot furrowed with worry for Edmund, enduring first the death of his son, terrible for any parent, then drifting from his wife and pressuring her terribly until she agreed to try anything he wanted to save their marriage and try to bring him out of his depression, and now perpetuating this terrible nonsense, the ridiculous idea that Shane was back.

Dot not settled, not content. The same DNA did not require the same name. Dot adamant but silent, Dot feeling this decision and this moniker were disrespectful of the perfect child whom she'd held and loved and lost and mourned. Dot doubtful, not looking down at the baby in the cradle, not gazing filled with love, but examining it like a licked finger coated in dust from a long-neglected surface. Dot despising the resemblance to her oldest grandson, the not-quite-perfect match: Shane with a birthmark under his left ear, this child without. Dot having disregarded the oft-repeated warnings, the cautioning to expect variations: the damnable orientation team making them watch that demented video with the six cows: all clones with the exact same DNA but distinct external markings, as each endured unique and differing conditions in the womb; only one, for example, with a black circle around its eye. Dot nauseated by the animated version of that cow—pathetically named Spot—cheerfully narrating the video.

Dot embodying that concept—differing conditions in the womb—herself a twin, having lived her life with a kind of clone, an exact genetic double, for whom she felt no great affinity beyond the surface, the purely physical. Dot examining the NeoKid™ now, unsurprised to feel revulsion, a subtle turning in her stomach, as though she'd eaten soft and runny eggs for breakfast. Dot not wanting to pick it up.

Him. Not wanting to pick him up.

Dot determined despite herself to care about this child, give it grandmotherly devotion, force herself to ignore her instincts and misgivings and to love this innocent baby, a baby so like Shane, and yet, not Shane at all.

CHRIS

Chris knew comics from the time he was born, growing up surrounded by shelves stacked with the thin spines of serial adventure and superpower, flipping through the fantastic pictures long before he could read, his father tucking him in with stories of spider bites and secret identities instead of the boring picture books they had at school. Chris creating, every blanket a cape, every scrap of clothing a costume, every hat a magic helmet, every cardboard box a lair or Batmobile or top-secret jet. Chris knowing that the comics came from someone else, a benefactor unseen, a person or entity named Daniel who had written that name inside each of the covers, though some had SUMEN scrawled in a less legible hand, mysterious: the Superheroes United to Maintain Earth's Nature, or the Society of Unlawful Monsters and Evil Nemeses?

Chris turning eight, a party with his friends, two cakes, one shaped like Superman and one like Wonder Woman, his two favourites, the rec room spinning with sugar and the raging wars of supervillains and heroes. Chris not noticing that his parents seemed nervous after everyone left, preoccupied with some adult concern; Chris curious as they sat him down before they even did the dishes or cleared the clutter and said they had to tell him something big, something about his comic collection and who Daniel was and what had happened before he was born.

Victim Services

Chris comforted to know that he was special, had a secret past, that he came into the world constructed as a copy of a boy who came before. Chris cavorting gleefully, ecstatic to discover his own Origins story: Chris, like Wolverine, concocted in a Canadian lab by scientific scoundrels. Chris cherishing for the first time the tiny Canadian flag he'd always had on his shoulder, understanding now it was not a birthmark but a tattoo, a badge, a mark of honour. Like Batman, like Robin, like the Green Lantern, like so many of his heroes, Chris was a person playing a part larger than himself, a role: his parents' son, who would try not to meet the tragic fate his predecessor had. Chris devoting himself to his destiny, his journey, his heroic path to find, learning lessons from the literature he inherited from Daniel, the stories Daniel left behind to guide Chris on his way.

SUMEN/PAMU

Sumen hitting the streets at sixteen, rucksack packed, refusing to look back, escaping in the neon night on the fast track to independent freedom. Sumen sleeping in alleys, curled up comfortable beneath the car-heavy overpass, tucked inside cardboard shanties in layer upon layer of fleecy clothing found at the Goodwill, Sally Ann, sleeping on buses, train station benches, sleeping fitfully in parks, in rundown squatter buildings, no electricity, no heat. Sumen travelling west in winter, to where the climate was warmer, Sumen riding the rails, hitchhiking, walking uncharted trails, eking out a meagre life in unfettered desperate terms.

Sumen changing his name to Pamu: Pamu of the Pavement, Pamu of the Park, Pamu far from the parents who had called him what they did. Called him Sumen for the past, called him Sumen for another son who died before his time. Pamu hating what he was, hating science, hating grief, his own dead sibling-self, the Sumen from before that they wanted him to be, smiling from pictures, grinning from the grave, Sumen who was different from what Pamu had inside.

Pamu having to leave them, to put it all behind. Pamu promising every star he'd never satisfy his parents with his presence or his news, his whereabouts, his goings-on, his friendship or his dreams. Pamu knowing they wanted him to be their son that died, to be what Sumen would have been if he had lived past nine. Pamu vowing that clone or not, his life would be his own.

5 The Failure of Justice

JANET & MARILYN

Janet and Marilyn standing silent at the front of the flower-filled church, stone-faced, the service spinning all around them like the fragments of a dream. Janet and Marilyn, shock sheltering them by sluicing emotion away from their bodies into some spiritual cistern they somehow shared, would draw on later, or drown in; bereavement barrelling them through ritual so fast they had no time to bombard their God with questions, to rage against their plight: burying their child—their heart, their love, their everything—first Michael at nine and now again his copy, their second love, Micah, at barely seventeen. *Lesbian Mothers Lose Son Twice* the headlines ran, Marilyn fuming at the word "lose," as though their negligence had caused this, as though they deserved it, as though they were distracted or careless as opposed to diligent, vigilant, near assiduous with their son. Marilyn seething, staring at those gathered in the church, daring them to judge her, condemn her, seeing only sympathy and grief gazing back at her but feeling they thought her a failure, how couldn't they, all the important people who'd given them their child back, the other NeoKid™ parents who hadn't lost their second chances, the lesbian community and queer rights councils and groups who since her youth had fought for her right to conceive and parent and had later used the press around the NeoKids™ to turn her and Janet into heroes, leading marches and rallies and parades, all those positive messages about queer parents somehow undercut now by his death, their negligence, her shame. Marilyn blaming herself because there was no one else: no drunk driver, no alcohol, no errant deer, no rowdy passengers or blaring music or even inexperienced error, just chance, just fate, just rotten bad luck: two cars and some ice—that was all it took to destroy his life, a second life so real and joyful they had taken for granted it would last longer than theirs.

Janet angry there weren't more of them, Marilyn surprised at how many had come—fifteen NeoKids™ here to grieve. Not that many of them were friends with Micah anymore, but they kept in touch, those who knew what they were, an online social network group and yearly get-togethers—the others having moved away, some of them to other ends of the country, and some who didn't know. Only four of them had stayed at the same school, including Micah, the others too afraid to go back into that building, that classroom, though they knew that was ridiculous—fear is stronger than logic, superstition is a hard master, and Marilyn felt it gripping her hard, pushing her down, threatening to invade every thought and action.

Janet looking almost longingly at the Mounties, those fine young men, lining the aisle like poppies, regal and red and ramrod straight, buttons gleaming, boots polished, standing like statues to honour the dead. Her dead. Janet scanning the sea of faces, the NeoKids™ in a row right near the front, outfits coordinated by God-knows-who, in charcoal grey, dresses for the girls, suits for the boys, six of whom had been weeping pallbearers, carrying her son towards her in the church, behind them scientists and government officials, Janet unable to remember their names, not the prime minister but his deputy, and a bunch of the officials from the Department of Justice, the founders of the NeoKid™ project. Janet shifting her gaze to some of the other parents: Gordon and June as silent and still as she and Marilyn; Kiyoma keening all in black, screaming grief and sobbing, surely thinking of her own son who had run away and refused to come back; and then the mobs of people she didn't know, heartfelt faces of sorrow which she'd been told extended outside the church and lined the sidewalks for city blocks. Janet wishing she could see each one of them, wishing she could fly, look down at all the people who came to pay respect to her only son. And what would happen now? Could they clone him again? Janet shaking, spasms erupting, the emotion reaching her body now, both of them too old for another baby to grow inside and Janet knowing, really knowing: it was finished; it was done.

LUCIEN

Lucien is the Monitor Man.

Lucien sitting in the chair shaped exactly to the contours of his ass, sitting in it every day for the past twenty-one years despite the days he technically gets off, according to his contract, which Lucien never takes. Lucien never travels, Lucien never stays home sick, Lucien's never late. He's the Monitor Man—the last original employee of the Guardian Angel Team.

When the project first went forward, from Victim Services, his superiors had been strict about the process: everything scrutinized, standardized, checked and double-checked, documented in both official languages and in triplicate. Lucien making history here, making Canada the world leader in cloning and reproductive therapy, Lucien Despres, geeky kid from Rimouski, making something of his life, not as a scientist but as a translator, assigned to the project full time with the "English girl" Julia Shaw as soon as the bill went through. Lucien transcribing, translating, observing, and recording, not meant to contribute or suggest, but Lucien spoke his mind often, spewing ideas that were impossible, ridiculous, scientifically unsound. But the one suggestion, the one flourish of design, the one flash of artistic genius, the one which they'd allowed, was the tattoos, each NeoKid™ tattooed on their left shoulder (boys) or their left hip (girls), with a small Canadian flag no bigger than a stamp. Lucien lunging across the table, saying the Canadian flag was already the most popular tattoo in Canada, saying the children wouldn't seem "marked" in an overly unusual way, new children with nothing to distinguish them as clones, nothing to set them apart or get them picked on in school, other than a tiny tattoo, under which was Lucien's pièce de résistance, a microchip that allowed the Guardian Angel Team to monitor vital signs and GPS location by satellite, a modification to which all the parents had agreed.

Lucien loving his reward for coming up with the idea, a position on the original surveillance team, the team beginning its real work when the NeoKids™ were finally given over to their parents. Most of the time that meant just sitting in front of a monitor, cycling between the twenty-eight different children, monitoring heart rate, life signs, and, if needed, geographical location: Omar (orig. Hashi) went through a phase of wandering off in public places when he was about six, and Salito (orig. Luco) got lost in a small boat when he was twelve, off the shores of PEI on a family vacation, the volunteer at the coast guard telling Lucien it was unlikely they would have found Sal at all if it hàdn't been for the GPS, making Lucien proud. Lucien almost losing his mind five years later, when Micah (orig. Michael) died, Lucien too distraught to attend the funeral, Lucien hating hardest the monitor, which had twenty-eight slots on it, with one now permanently dark.

Lucien likes the nights the best, when he gets to work alone. Every now and then, in the early hours of the morning, when the city is even and quiet, Lucien hears a gentle knock and opens up his door. There is a woman waiting there, and Lucien knows her name, knows Sumen is her son. She comes in and removes her coat, while Lucien returns to his chair. He switches all the monitors to the signals from her boy, so that they can hear the electronic blips that represent his life, just to listen, just to know that he's all right. Lucien watches as this mother shuts her eyes, swaying back and forth to the beeps and boops of her son's healthy beating heart, awash in the glowing comfort of the screen.

Victim Services

THE DIVINITY GENE

JESI (FROM POPLOPEDIA, THE ORIGINAL FREE ENCYCLOPEDIA)
The term **Jesi** refers to any of the viable human offspring created from the **DNA** formula released by **Dr. Maciej Wawrzyniec** on October 17th, 2006, at 9:57 PM (GMT), believed to be the accurate genetic code of **Jesus of Nazareth** (see also **Jesus Christ**). The term can include the miraculous or biological descendants of Jesi, although the latter are also referred to as **demi-Jesi/semi-Jesi, quadrajeez, octajeez**, etc.

ORIGINS OF THE JESI

Dr. Maciej Wawrzyniec, a **Polish geneticist** who attended the **International Academy for the Advancement of Science** between 1962 and 1968, posted a 144-page document to no less than eighteen known internet forums at 9:57 PM on October 17th of 2006. Referred to as **The Post**, this document had been downloaded over 80,000 times by 6:00 AM the following morning. The first section of the document

expanded upon his research into the standard cloning pro-
cedures of the early millennium (see **somatic cell nuclear
transfer**), and outlined his instructions for how to choose
the suitable woman to carry the **Second Coming of Christ**.
The second section of the document, in ninety-eight pages,
gave the full genetic sequence for the DNA of Jesus Christ.

The cloning method proposed by Dr. Wawrzyniec and
later practised by several private companies, national gov-
ernments, and educational organizations, now known as
the **Dr. W. Method**, requires an **egg donor surrogate mother**.
One percent of the offspring's DNA, the **mitochondrial DNA**,
therefore belongs to the mother. Dr. Wawrzyniec's document outlined criteria for selecting the **New Mary** (see also
Semper Virgin, Mulier Amicta Sole), including genetic history, IQ, religious affiliation, age, sexual history, and "moral
orthodoxy." His wishes were ignored.

By November 23, 2006, the **Newcastle Centre for Life
(United Kingdom)**, the **Microsoft Corporation (United
States)**, Professor **Hwang Woo-suk (South Korea)**, and the
national government of **Russia** had each announced their
intentions to generate one clone of Christ. The women chosen to carry these four original clones were kept under
twenty-four-hour surveillance and medical care, and the
video feed of each woman during the duration of her pregnancy was broadcast over the internet (for archives of the
videos, see **www.watchthejesi.org/archives**). Under the
aegis of the **United Nations**, many world leaders made
statements against the cloning of Christ, the most vocal of
whom was **President Bush** of the **United States of America**
(click **here** for a copy of his speech). After the events of the
Munich Miracle (see below), this outcry against the cloning
stopped. Dr. Wawrzyniec had become the most recognizable name on the planet (though, as the North American

Consolidated Press quipped that December, still the hardest to pronounce). He had, however, disappeared from the public arena by then and become a recluse. He had no further known involvement in the development of the Jesi.

The source DNA for the Jesi remains a subject of some controversy, and as Dr. Wawrzyniec never revealed how he procured his base genetic sample, nothing definitive can be said. There is consensus, however, in scientific, religious, and academic circles, that the DNA used was indeed that of the historical Christ.

BIRTH, EARLY LIFE, AND PROPAGATION OF THE JESI

The first Jesus was born in July of 2007, to the South Korean mother (for the birth dates of the other Jesi, click **here**). According to the doctors present, the mother did experience the normal pain of childbirth, but the baby did not cry. Ethnically, the baby appeared **Middle Eastern**. Three days after the South Korean Jesus was born an assassin successfully shot the mother, although the shooter missed the child. A witness held the silent child to his mother's side, and the baby suckled at her breast. Reportedly, the woman's wounds were healed and she returned to life. Many dismissed this as global myth, however later events imply it may well be true. The assassin evaded capture, and no group or individual has ever claimed responsibility.

The four original Jesi grew and learned at an accelerated speed, which was unexpected. According to the **four Biblical Gospels**, the original Christ had grown as a normal child. The Jesi appeared adolescent after only one year. This may have been due to an imperfection in the cloning process (see **Dolly the sheep, premature aging,** and **telomeres**). When questioned about it, the Jesi all gave the same answer; they simply responded: "Things have been changed." Other than

The Divinity Gene

162

the incident in South Korea, no miraculous behaviour was noted during the first two years of life. After several articles about the **Divinity Gene** and coverage of the drastic increase in pressure from anti-reproductive technology activists to prevent future instances of human cloning, the media buzz died down somewhat. Public interest in the Jesi resumed in May of 2009, when the **British Jesus** showed his capacity for granting **miracles**.

At a photo op with **Prince Harry**, the British Jesus (named **Hugh** at the request of his surrogate mother, a fan of British actor **Hugh Grant**) was approached by a tearful woman of Argentinian descent, pleading that she was a "pure vessel" meant to carry a Christ-child. The Jesus touched her and said, "**It is done.**" She reportedly took three pregnancy tests that afternoon, all of which came back positive. On February 14, 2010, **Valeria Paz** gave birth to the first **Miraculous Jesus**. (Gestational time of Jesi embryos is not accelerated, for unknown reasons.)

Following the successful fertilization of Valeria Paz, many women the world over sought to be impregnated in a miraculous manner by the various Jesi. For approximately the first year it was standard for the "**Pilgrim Wombs**"—women who sought to carry a Jesus clone—to be virgins, due to the Catholic doctrine that holds that the mother of Jesus Christ conceived without having sexual intercourse (see **Virginal Conception**). When it became clear, however, that the Jesi would grant pregnancy to anyone who asked for it, women of any sexual history or creed became mothers of Jesi using the miraculous method.

By June 2013, it was estimated that there were at least seven hundred existent Jesi, and the numbers have grown exponentially from that point forward. All of the known Jesi are male. Jesi conceived miraculously show the same advanced rate of aging as the cloned Jesi, for unknown reasons. Before the age of twelve (the equivalent of the mid-thirties in a normal human male), the Jesi are often sexually active, and many have reproduced biologically. These unions have thus created **hybrid Jesus-human children**, and have irreversibly mixed the **Jesus DNA** into that of the human species. Given the miraculous capabilities of the Jesi (discussed below), many prominent members of the scientific community have come to accept the theory of **Intelligent Design** in some form, and to regard the addition of the Jesus DNA as the most significant advance in human **evolution** since *homo erectus* became **bipedal**.

MIRACULOUS CAPABILITIES OF THE JESI

The first known miracle enacted by a Jesi, with the possible exception of the resurrection of the South Korean **birth mother** (see above), is the impregnation of Valeria Paz (see **propagation of the Jesi**, above). After this event, the four Jesi became celebrity figures in their own countries and worldwide, performing miracles in public.

The first instance of healing the sick (the **Munich Miracle**) occurred at a long-term care facility in **Munich, Germany**. No media representatives were present at the event, but later accounts from witnesses confirm that on June 3, 2009, no less than seven Jesi converged at the facility at 3:00 AM, arriving on foot. (It was later speculated that the Jesi **teleported** to Germany, a power they have since demonstrated on countless occasions.)

The Jesi restored mobility, speech, and muscle mass to three men: **Hermann Gottlieb, Paolo Abbaggio**, and **Henri Dauphin**. All three men were quadriplegics with reduced brain function, as the result of ingesting an unidentified toxin in 1964, while students at the International Academy for the Advancement of Science. The fact that the three injured men had attended the academy concurrently with Dr. Wawrzyniec did not go unnoticed. Internet discussion boards were filled with speculation: about the role of the academy in the invention of the cloning process and the procurement of the base genetic sample; about whether or not Dr. Wawrzyniec may have been exposed to the toxin but been genetically immune (see **survivor's guilt**), whether he may have created the toxin, or whether he had any extraordinary knowledge of the toxin at all; and about the three men themselves—their personal histories, nationalities, and fields of research before paralysis.

The possible reasons for the miracle were not explored in depth outside of the blogosphere, however, as most mainstream media chose to focus on the fact that seven Jesi had been sighted in Munich, when only four were known to have been created. Privately funded investigation and media pressure for the responsible parties to come forward, as well as questioning of the Jesi themselves, led to the admission that Jesi had been created clandestinely by the **Coca-Cola Company** in **Fort Oglethorpe, Georgia**, and, with the assistance of unsanctioned government funds, at the **Harvard Stem Cell Institute** in the United States and the **Tehran University of Medical Sciences** in **Iran**.

In 2010, the seven Jesi walked across the Strait of Georgia in British Columbia, Canada, carrying torches and inaugurating the xxi Olympic Winter Games in Vancouver.

The first case of **resurrection** occurred in 2011, after a suicide bomber detonated explosives strapped to her chest while hugging the **Microsoft Jesus** in **Israel**. His final words were "**And so it is done.**" The world went into mourning.

The other Jesi refused to make any comment on the death of their brother. Three days later, however, the Microsoft

Jesus showed up for his scheduled function at a hospital in Palestine. When questioned he simply said, with one of the few genuine looks of surprise ever recorded on a Jesus, "**And on the third day, I rise again.**" Faith in the Jesi increased, including a dramatic rise in the number of ordained religious leaders, and the total number of Jesi-bearing pregnancies (both miraculous and biological) more than doubled.

LETHARGY OF THE JESI

An unexpected phenomenon associated with the Jesi is the utter lethargy and unresponsiveness that sets in approximately ten to twelve years after birth. The term "**zombie-god**" has been used by more than one commentator, though "**lethargized Jesi**" is now considered the proper designation. The lethargized Jesi follow simple instructions if asked, but they do not speak, nor eat nor drink, nor respond to requests for miracles.

The lethargy of the Jesi is what led to their eventual enslavement. The first widespread use of the Jesi was in minefields. After the assassination attempt in Israel (and several others that followed) it became clear that the Jesi could not be killed. A full-blooded Jesus in the state of lethargy will respond only to simple commands (a half-blood, or demi-Jesus, tends to experience severe depression in later life, which can be treated with **conventional antidepressants**). When asked to walk through a known minefield, a lethargic Jesus will comply. When the land mines detonate, the Jesi are generally destroyed, but will return to the field three days later.

Once the Jesi began their **demining** work in **Afghanistan, Eritrea, Ethiopia, Serbia**, and along the **Thai-Burmese border**, the **civil rights controversy** concerning the humanity of the lethargized Jesi became a high-profile international

The Divinity Gene

issue. The debate is ongoing: **the UN legal unit** works tirelessly in the defence of the lethargized Jesi, but because of the sheer number of them there is little that can be done. Lethargic Jesi are most often used for dangerous work such as demining, demolition, and working on offshore oil rigs. In the early phases of lethargy, the Jesi are often used in hospital emergency rooms to heal fatal traumas. Other contested commercial uses for lethargized Jesi include medical testing, pharmaceutical research, and military development. It is also believed that organized crime rings have abducted lethargized Jesi and sold them into prostitution, used them to create counterfeit currency, and forced them to perpetrate torture and commit murder.

GOD-CONSCIOUSNESS AND RELIGIOSITY OF THE JESI

A long-standing theological question in various **Christian** sects has been the original Christ's possession of **God-consciousness**, the total and complete knowledge of his **divine personality**. The Jesi have never commented on this issue nor any other aspect of religious doctrine, despite requests from literally every leader of a **world religion**. To date they have refused to engage in any kind of formal religious teaching at all, including the telling of **parables**, for which the original Christ is renowned. They will not make any absolute statements about faith or the specifics of the **afterlife**. When questioned, they tend to simply say "**All that has been said before.**" Their patience is indefatigable and they are never caught in any kind of rhetorical trick. Another characteristic possibly related to God-consciousness is that all the Jesi have been (and continue to be) perfectly multilingual in every known language, living or dead, including sign languages, pidgins, creoles, and regional dialects, regardless of lack of exposure in their early childhoods.

At various points in the past thirty-five years, religious groups have responded to the Jesi with denial, outrage, acceptance, paranoia, obsession, and devotion. The sheer range of reactions exceeds the parameters of this article, from proclaiming certain Jesi as godheads to denouncing all Jesi as idols. (See **the Papacy, Protestant Christian reactions, Judaic reactions, Islamic reactions, Hindu reactions, other religious influences of the Jesi**, etc.)

IMPLICATIONS AND AFTER-EFFECTS OF THE JESI

The implications of the existence of Jesi in terms of sustainable human population growth and gender equality in the species are largely unknown. However, given the seemingly limitless power the Jesi have in early life, there seems to be a consensus that no single problem will prove insurmountable.

In May 2020, in **Poland**, the remains of Dr. Maciej Wawrzyniec were discovered by a tourist who had gotten lost during an "extreme hiking" tour in the mountains. Autopsy confirmed that he died of exposure to the cold. On his person was a handwritten note dated December 2009, part of which read "You have desecrated the one true thing that ever existed, and made my life's work profane." The death was ruled a suicide, as the note went on to give instructions for the disposal of his body should it ever be found. In accordance with his wishes, he has not been resurrected.

[*last updated June 18, 2029*]

2.

Last year was a good year for me—I made it into *People's* hundred sexiest men alive issue for the third time, became the world's seventeenth youngest billionaire, and was interviewed by Barbara Walters as one of 2006's most fascinating

The Divinity Gene

people. You might have seen the interview: Barbara said, "Convince me that you awe not as despicable as evwyone thinks," and I said, "Barbara, I'm much more despicable than most people can even imagine, and that doesn't bother me at all." That line got quoted a lot. And then of course there was my profile in the *New Yorker:* "Jordan Shaw and his Cabinet of Human Atrocities."

This year, things are taking a drastic turn for the worse. It's the dreams I've been having. Real horrifying shit. Angels on meat hooks getting their guts torn out and ground up into sausages. Packs of black dogs ripping old people apart in the hospital while the nurses watch and laugh. I wake up with my heart pounding like I've just done an eight-ball of coke, and if there's one thing I'm still scared of in this world it's dying alone in my bed.

It's destroying my life. I can't hold erections, I can't keep down any solid food, let alone the rich stuff I normally eat, and I haven't taken a photograph in months. It's guilt, plain and simple. And that's the fucking kicker. I'm as Catholic as the day I was confirmed. No matter how much blow I snort, no matter how many Sundays I sit home with my thumb up my ass, no matter how many dumb-ass blondes I stick my dick into, I'm still an altar boy at heart.

And dumb as a box of hair. Shit.

I DON'T BELIEVE in god. I *don't.* My mother started me off Catholic, kneeling all the time, worrying rosary beads like rubbing them would make her life any better than it was, constantly muttering prayers to her magic man in the sky. She kept a strict home, so we weren't supposed to even *think* about touching meat on Fridays. Not even fish—she didn't want to take chances. Every Friday we had mashed potatoes, boiled turnips, and baked beets. You can imagine what a treat that was for a kid.

So one Friday when I was nine years old, I took all the quarters I'd been saving for a couple of months, and after dinner I pretended I was going to a friend's place and headed straight to Burger King. I bought the most gorgeous, juicy Whopper you've ever seen and bit into all that beef, clear grease and ketchup all over my face. On the way home I had to pass by Our Lady of Perpetual Help. I was scared shitless, thinking god was going to strike me down for transgressing his laws and walking right past his doorstep. And nothing happened. I licked my lips and I knew then that my mother was an idiot and that god didn't exist. I don't remember anything else that went through my head, but I got my first hard-on, a real stiffy in my jeans. Just the little kid kind, but it was my own little miracle.

Barbara Walters asked me when I first became fascinated with human evil. Was it when I worked developing crime scene photos for the NYPD? When I started taking my own photos in less developed countries? I fed her some bull about studying the holocaust in high school, and having a friend who'd been the victim of abuse from a stepfather.

And when, she wanted to know, did I dedicate myself to the pursuit of exotic physical pleasure? When I made my first million at the age of twenty-six? When my stocks in antidepressant medications tripled? I told her my body is the only thing I know for sure is real, the only thing I trust, and physical pleasure is the only happiness I really understand. Did I identify as a hedonist? Not exactly. Just someone who likes to have monthly caviar hot tub parties, spleen massages, orgies. Don't I need some kind of higher gratification, for my mind or, dare she say it, soul? I don't believe in the

The Divinity Gene

soul, nothing eternal about me. And for my mind I have my photography. Although I see it as a kind of visual pleasure, not so distinct from my purely physical delights. Isn't it contradictory, then, that I'm most well known for photographing holy religious relics? No, Barbara, not at all. They're very beautiful, and in some ways they are exactly the same as the things I collect myself. "Ah," said Barbara, off camera, "I've promised my producers not to mention your abominable collection."

THE NEW YORKER guy didn't even pretend to like me. I could see the look of disgust on his face the whole time, and I kind of got off on it. When he went to shake my hand at the end of the interview, which we had in my apartment so he could see all my pieces, I shot my hand forward and grabbed his wrist, hard. His eyes widened a bit and he looked scared, and I leaned forward and kissed him. I could tell he was a fag. I told him if he gave me fifty bucks he could blow me. He said no, acted offended, but I could tell he was thinking about it. That's the shit I love. That's humanity. I don't really like sex with guys, but I don't mind it, either. The closest I've ever come to transcendence is when I'm blowing my load, preferably in someone's face. And if that someone is a preppy-looking Ivy League journalist fag who hates himself for paying to blow someone he finds morally repulsive but physically attractive—well, that's just pure gold. I wish I had a picture of him licking my spunk off his lips.

He didn't mention it in the article, of course. He omitted a lot of things. "The Cabinet of Human Atrocities"—that was his name for my collection, but he left most of the good things out. Things he mentioned: the elephant foot stool with the zebra skin seat cover; all the ivory; the gorilla hand ashtray; two of the illegal meals I've eaten and photographed (manatee steak and panda veal); some of the serial killer stuff I've collected; the Aztec human sacrifice artefacts; and, surprisingly, the blanched skull of a Tutsi man that I smuggled out of Rwanda in '94. Things he didn't mention in the article: all the Nazi memorabilia (that surprised me); my copies of the Bernardo tapes; the pickled body parts from Ground Zero and my piece of shrapnel from the second plane; and my prize possession—the one from Poland. He didn't ask me any of the questions I usually get when people see that: how does it work, what happens if I unplug it, am I ever going to try to wake the kid up. This guy didn't even ask me how I got it, and given what I've learned since, I wouldn't have told him.

MY PHOTOGRAPHS OF holy relics are just the public face of what I do. I photograph lots of things: concentration camps (my favourite is a piece of graffiti in Kaunas Fort IX reading *If God exists, he's going to have to beg ME for forgiveness*), that theatre in Russia where the government gassed the entire audience just to take out the Chechen terrorists inside, mass graves, all that kind of stuff. And porn you need to see to believe. Lots of people know about what I do, the kind of things I like to collect. I'm not a good candidate for religious photography.

Back in 1991 I was travelling around South America, chewing coca leaves, looking for torture devices on the black market, trying to bang as much Latin pussy as I could. In Chile I ate a traditional indigenous dish similar to *cabrito guisado*: they slit the throat of a live goat and let the blood pour into a pan loaded with garlic and herbs. When the blood congeals, it's sliced and served, like Jell-O. It had been technically illegal since the eighties, thanks to a law the

The Divinity Gene

city-bred animal rights activists pushed through, but in the mountains no one cares. When I got to Venezuela I wound up in a little town called Betania, in the arms of a television journalist named Sonia Mañana, with long straight hair and perky tits. I wanted to spend the Christmas holidays in bed with her, so on December 8 I let her drag me to church for some feast day. I wouldn't have gone for anyone else in the world, but she had the best ass I've ever had the pleasure to be inside of. I was only twenty-three years old, and couldn't help myself.

The cathedral was Gothic and stunning as shit, and I spent my hour walking around at the back, tuning out what was going on up front, studying the architecture and the stained glass, surreptitiously taking pictures. It had been a long time since I'd been inside a church, and I realized I'd been missing out on some very pleasing, gory, artwork. In one of the side altars, they had a bloodied piece of gauze that supposedly came from the side of Archbishop Romero when he was assassinated in El Salvador in 1980. How it ended up in Venezuela I'm not sure, but I was fascinated by it because it looked exactly like something I had in my collection at home: a t-shirt sprayed with blood that I'd bought off a kid who'd been beaten up at school by his brother and his friends. Next thing I know, there's a scream from behind me, and I turn to see a nun yelling that the host is bleeding.

I snapped a picture. If you were to look at this picture now, you would see a rosy glow like the aurora borealis all around the host. Sure, it's weird, but it's not a miracle. I can show you any number of pictures I've taken in my kitchen or my backyard with similar wonky lighting effects. It could have been bad film. It could have been a reflection. It could have been anything.

The priest quieted everyone down and went back to saying the Mass, but when he finished no one would leave. They all just sat there, praying. I saw Sonia give me the look of death, so I just kept lurking on the sidelines waiting for something to happen. A few hours later the priest brought out the host, and I had my Nikon 570 ready. This part is true: that host dripped blood into the chalice like the priest was squeezing an orange. And I got it all on Kodak 35mm ISO 800 film.

Since then, people keep asking me: Jordan, you saw the miracle, how can you not believe? It's such a profoundly stupid question. I don't know what happened in that church, but I don't think it was divine. I've seen monks in Asia do weirder things than make bread bleed. And I haven't joined any of their honky-tonk religions.

This is what happens next: Sonia never touches me again—she becomes this totally hardcore devoted Catholic. The priest takes the host to Bishop Pio Bello Ricardo of Los Teques. The bishop sends it to "experts" at the medical institute in Caracas for analysis. The experts come back with the following information: the red substance on the host *is* blood of human origin, containing red and white corpuscles, and doesn't match the priest. The blood stays fluid for three days, then begins to dry up, leaving a small red spot at the centre of the host. The host stays totally dry on one side— the blood doesn't go through it. I sell my photos to *Time* for $75,000, which makes my name as a photographer of relics and miraculous phenomena. This leads, eventually, to Petr Grabowicz.

IN 1995 I was in Italy. I was there for my own reasons—Nero, gladiatorial relics, Pompeii—but also photographing the supposed Eucharistic miracle at Lanciano. Catholics believe that during the Mass the bread and wine change, not in form but in "essence," into the body and blood of Christ, and that when they eat and drink of these they receive the whole Christ—body, blood, soul, and divinity. "Miracles" like the one I saw in Betania and the one in Lanciano prove and reaffirm this doctrine for them. And pictures of it sell like smut.

I had some trouble after Venezuela—the Church got wind of who I was and didn't want me poking around all their sacred bits of flesh and snapping photos. What saved me was a bishop in Mexico permitting me to photograph some relics there six months later. The reason he allowed me is because I happened to know he was screwing two sisters and supporting children with each of them, which I discovered by fucking Lucia while he was with Mercedes. He issued a pastoral letter about me, saying: "God has been revealing Himself and his Truth to mankind through flawed instruments since Creation, and the Church has always held these messages to be True and superior to the flaws and human failings of those who bear them. The Mystery and the Power of any Holy Relic cannot be tarnished by being photographed or recorded by any man-made technology, and the morality of the photographer is certainly irrelevant. Such pictures can only serve to further evangelize and spread the Word of Christ." After that, no bishop ever denied me access to anything.

The relics at Lanciano are the granddaddy of Eucharistic miracles. They supposedly date back to 700 AD, when a monk named St. Legontian doubted the presence of Christ in the Eucharist. One morning, at consecration, he was shocked to discover the host change into flesh, and the wine change into blood. The relics were placed into an ivory tabernacle and guarded by the monks. They hardened but they never decayed.

THE DIVINITY GENE

175

In the seventies, a priest decided to have them tested by science. Dr. Odoardo Linoli, a university professor-at-large and head physician of the united hospitals at Arezzo did a series of tests, and verified everything with Dr. Ruggero Bertelli from the University of Siena. They found: the relics are real flesh and blood of human origin; the flesh consists of the muscular tissue of the heart; the blood from both samples is A B positive. They did not find any evidence of preservatives or mummification techniques.

So in 1995 some priest wanted to write a book about the whole thing in English, and hired me to take the pictures. End of story.

Except: my second night there I was in the hotel bar drinking scotch that was older than I was when a man in his late forties with fly-away hair approached me. Sometimes I get recognized; there's a small circle of people around the world who collect the same kind of macabre things I'm into, or sometimes it's a human rights activist who thinks I'm deplorable, or sometimes it's someone who thinks they have something I want. I'm always a little bit wary, but this guy was different. There was an air about him—not quite menacing, but it certainly didn't put me at ease.

I asked him what he wanted, and he said, just like it was nothing, "I want to steal part of the relics of Lanciano."

I was surprised, to say the least. I'm not known for crime. I've broken laws, sure, in terms of smuggling or hunting endangered species, but I've never outright stolen anything—I've never had to. But it made sense to me immediately—I would have access to the relics in order to photograph them, and anyone who wanted to find out could have known that. I sat back and let him talk.

"I'm not going to tell you my name, nor what I want with the relics." He had a heavy eastern European accent I

The Divinity Gene

couldn't place, though I thought it might be Czech. "I don't need very much of them, so little in fact that no one will ever know." He took a clear plastic dish like an earplug container out of his pocket, and a metal instrument that looked like it belonged to a dentist. "You will find a way to remove the glass surrounding the relics, and you will scrape the flesh and the blood into this dish. Scrape very lightly—I only need a little of the material—but make sure it is visible to your eye. Don't gouge the relics—I want you to treat them with the greatest reverence, no matter what you believe. Bring me the dish, and your work will be done."

"Why should I?"

His eyes narrowed and hardened a little. "I know who you are, Mr. Shaw, and I know what kind of thing it is that interests you. You have more money than I could ever hope to provide you with. But I have something to offer you which I do not think you will able to refuse."

"What's that?"

"First, a plant of my own creation. I am a geneticist. I have created a plant that is a hybrid of tobacco, marijuana, and coca plants. I believe you will find the effects when ingested most unique and most pleasurable."

"That sounds great, but you know it's not nearly enough. Second?"

"Have you heard about the Petr Grabowicz case?"

I was surprised for the second time. Of course I knew what he was referring to. Anyone who collects the kinds of things I do pays close attention to the international news. Just a few weeks before arriving in Italy I'd been fishing around near Kassel, Germany, where a man advertised online that he wanted to eat someone, and received a response from another man looking to be eaten. The two met, had sex, then cooked and ate the one man's penis—all the while videotaping the spectacle. Then the newly castrated man was killed—according to his wishes—and his new friend continued to dine on him until the incident was discovered by police, investigating tips from internet users who had seen the suspicious postings. The best part was that the cops had a hard time pressing charges at first because the whole thing was consensual, with signatures to prove it. I was trying to buy the dishes and cutlery they'd used, but someone else snatched those up before I could talk to the right people. All I ended up with was a static-ridden copy of the videotape.

But Petr Grabowicz, he was a six-year-old kid who had died three months earlier in Poland. In a little town near the German border called Świnoujście, a homeless person dressed up as a fairy and walked onto a pond where the local children were skating. He told them he was the pond fairy, and if they didn't give him money he would cause the ice to melt so they would fall in. When the kids didn't buy it, he cut a hole in the ice, grabbed one of the boys from the pond, and drowned him.

"What about it?" I asked the self-proclaimed geneticist. He leaned into me and whispered into my ear. By the time he finished my heart was pounding. I looked at him, and he stared right back at me, expressionless. I finally asked, "So why do you want these relics so badly?"

"I've told you not to ask. I don't approve of your collection, but I think I understand the principle behind it. There was a time in my life when I wanted to use the wonders of the natural world to reveal God to the world. You are using the horrors of humanity to reveal the evil of the world. I'm a man of faith and science—and you are not. I'm doing this

The Divinity Gene

only because I believe it's for the greater good, and that if I am successful even you will come to see the light of true knowledge and redemption."

THE WHOLE HEIST appealed to my utter love of corruption. I arranged to photograph the relics one-on-one with the head priest of the parish, who balked when I asked him to remove the glass. When I told him I'd arrange for a sizeable donation to be given to his parish every year in perpetuity, provided he give me ten minutes alone with the relics, he lifted the case off and left. He came back ten minutes later, to the second. I'm not sure when he figured out I was lying about the money, but I never heard from him again.

The thing is, I didn't know the guy was going to do this fucked up shit with it. Cloning Christ. Apparently they've got four different women pregnant with freaky Christ babies. I knew he was crazy when he mentioned Grabowicz and cryogenic stasis units in the same sentence. But I thought he was just a religious nut who wanted to steal the holy relics so he could eat them or sell them on eBay. Harmless. But when that internet post went up last October, and everyone was all abuzz, I knew it was him. I knew what I'd done. And I knew everything was going to hell.

I haven't felt guilty for anything since I was nine years old. And now these dreams. Last night I was being eaten alive by locusts. Night before that I was in Africa, slicing open the distended bellies of starving kids, pulling out smooth gold stones and eating them. What's so frustrating about it is that I'm totally doing it to myself. I must be. I've been to every shrink in New York and some in Europe, but not one of them can make these dreams go away.

So God's finally won. I believe in you now, you prick. You've made my life a living hell and you've sent the dreams to drive me crazy. You want me to kneel down and pray? Fine, I can go and do that. But don't think for a second I buy your bullshit about forgiveness and eternal love—there's no repenting everything I've done. You're just a nasty son of a bitch who's holding all the cards and wants to see me squirm. But I'm still right about life. I'm still right about all of it.

3.

Magda Wawrzyniec, struggling with the weight of her swollen stomach onto bent knees, her skirt bunching slightly so that varicose veins show in her calves, the blue histories of the strain of her seven pregnancies, now eight, kneels at the prie-dieu before the monstrance and lights a candle for the soul encased inside her. She is praying Hail Marys, thinking of the Virgin and the greatness of what can fill a womb, praying that her own child—a son, she hopes, God's will be done—will do great things for the Glory of God. She is thankful that she has lived to see 1946, that many she loves have survived the terrible war, that her husband is alive.

When her prayers finish (she imagines them flying up to Heaven tied to the feet of doves, like the carrier pigeons her grandfather used to raise), she once again gets to her feet with the help of the railing, and begins her walk home. Just as she opens the church door and feels the cold night search and embrace her, she lurches and her shoes are suddenly wet. Her first thought, upon releasing her font onto the threshold of God's house, is that this might be a sin, and her second thought is *Dear God no please no not now it's much too soon.*

Consciousness ebbs away from her as her feet slide out from under, as the young priest with the mole on his cheek comes rushing out to answer what she realizes now are her screams. When she wakes up in the hospital they tell her it has been three days (impossible), that the baby is small and weak but expected, miraculously, to live, that she cannot have any more children. Her eyes flutter and she whimpers and they reassure her again that the baby is going to be fine (thank God), was born in the church, baptized Maciej Magnus, and given last rites.

She lets herself go under again, praising God, sending up a prayer of thanksgiving carried by six of the most beautiful doves, hallelujah, hallelujah.

MACIEJ'S FATHER IS considerably older than his wife. He was born in 1882 and apprenticed as a baker at fourteen, waking well before the sun and rolling dough to the rhythms of the rosary, saying the prayers in Latin for twelve hours each day. He has married twice and fathered fourteen children. His first family, his child bride and their six beautiful children, were knocked out by a bout of scarlet fever that he himself barely survived. Magda had saved him from his misery, and now, walking to bring her and the babe home from the hospital at last, he marvels at what a man can experience in sixty-odd years. Glory be to God.

His face is deeply creased, and his eyes widen with wonder as he reaches out for this son, who he knows will be his last and who almost did not exist at all. His forearms are marked with burn scars from years with the oven, and holding the sleeping Maciej he marvels at how pale and soft his son seems, as though he could knead him into a pretzel or a bagel or a hot cross bun, as though there were no bones or blood inside him, just soft, doughy flesh. His eyes are just two tiny raisins and yet Tomas sees something of himself there, like looking at a reflection in a dusty mirror.

Magda looks pale and tired and frail, and for a moment so much like his first wife Agnes that he cannot speak. When the moment passes he says, "Magda, thank you for our son. Thank you for Maciej." Magda smiles at him, and when their eyes meet he knows she will come through.

WHEN MAGDA DIES seven years later Tomas puts his fist through the drywall of their small two-bedroom apartment. This breaks his hand and he is unable to work at the bakery for a month. Sitting at his mother's funeral, Maciej thinks about his father's swollen hand and his mother's hands, how she used to run them through his hair when she put him to bed at night, and how now she cannot move them at all. He believes his mother still exists, in every way, but he does not understand why her spirit can no longer work to move her body. His father cannot move his right hand and his mother cannot move her right hand—the symptoms are the same but the causes are totally different. He makes a note to ask Father Krzysztof about this. He thinks about Christ and the Glory of the Resurrection. He will receive Confirmation this month.

Maciej is not sitting with the rest of his family on this solemn occasion. He has been an altar boy for a year now. This is something Magda was very proud of, beaming when she told the other mothers in their building and telling him that he was a good son when they were talking softly alone together. The family, and Father Krzysztof, thought it would honour Magda for Maciej to serve this role at her funeral Mass. His robe is scarlet, with a white cassock overtop, but he is careful to use the black sleeve of the shirt he is wearing underneath when he wipes away his tears.

Tomas's hand does not heal well, and as the month wears on things are getting tighter around the house: tone of voice, eyes, belts. Maciej's closest sibling is eight years older, and they are the only two children still living at home. Tomas is old and his hand does not heal and money is scarce, and so after two months Tomas goes to live with his eldest son and his wife, and the sister goes to live with her older sister and her husband, married three months before Magda died, but no one can take in a child of Maciej's age and appetite, and so he is sent to live with Father Krzysztof and the priests in the church where he was born. When he leaves Tomas lets tears stand in his eyes because he is sad to be separated from his son, but there is pride on his face because Maciej will honour God and this will honour their family.

MACIEJ IS THIRTEEN years old and kneeling in the church in handed-down pants that are shiny and thin at the knees, and he is contemplating the crucified Christ. He has sinned. He has, once, cheated on the German homework that Father Krzysztof insists he do. He has tried a cigarette he found while sweeping the church, smoked it in the lot behind the rectory. And twice in the past week he has given in to the flurry in his chest and the sweat in his palms and abused himself. These acts weigh upon him gravely, and he knows he must confess them. He gazes at Christ on the cross, the Face twisted with suffering, the Wounds bleeding, the Agony. How Christ suffered and died for the sins of Man, so that all might be redeemed. He thinks: *How much of that suffering am I personally responsible for?* And the answer comes to him as though his guardian angel has whispered it in his ear: *All of it.* Maciej gasps as he realizes the fundamental truth of this: even had Maciej been the only human being to ever live, Christ in His love would still have come down and suffered and died, for Maciej alone. Because it could have happened that way, it is as though it did happen that way. Maciej begins to weep.

FATHER KRZYSZTOF smiles and places his hand on Maciej's shoulder. "I'm not sending you *away*, little Francis, I am sending you *to* somewhere, *to* education, *to* a greater understanding of Creation." "My little Francis," after St. Francis of Assisi, is what Father Krzysztof has taken to calling Maciej, whose interest in the natural world, in how birds fly and animals run and how plants grow, whose interest in science has always been as unwavering as his faith. Maciej who always beamed when he learned of natural phenomena mirroring Revelation—the sand dollar, pale fragile discs with five holes to represent the five wounds of Christ; the Easter lily; the Passion Flower, again with five bleeding, wounded tips; the Crucifix catfish, *Arius proops*, in whose skulls men saw depictions of the crucified Christ, whose very bone structure contained a thorn from Christ's crown and the shape of a Roman soldier's shield, whose otoliths, small skull bones used for balance and discerning gravity, rattled in the dried skull to represent the dice used to gamble for Christ's clothes.

Maciej does not want to leave the church, his home, does not want to leave Poland. But he is obedient. "Will I become a priest or a scientist?" he asks Father Krzysztof, whom he wants to make proud. "How will I choose?"

THE ACADEMY LOOMS up from the German countryside like a blister, all glass and steel and chrome among rolling hills of tall grasses and wildflowers Maciej recognizes and knows well, both by their Latin names and for their symbolic relation to the Virgin Mary: eglantine and honeysuckle, aphananthe and gromwell, peonies and Job's Tears. It is 1962 and the tenth anniversary of the International Academy for the Advancement of Science. Only fifteen boys are selected each year, and Maciej is the only student from Poland, and the only Catholic. He stands at the gate with his single battered suitcase, a gift from Father Krzysztof, containing his few clothes, a wooden crucifix that had belonged to his mother, and his copy of *Lives of the Saints.* He presses the suitcase to his nose and tries to smell the church vestibule, the dust of the rectory, the liquid wax of the devotional candles, the thick incense of ritual. He smells only leather.

In his first year he takes the school-wide prize in genetics, for cross-pollinating a lady slipper orchid and a weeping birch. He names his creation *Cypripedium betula*, and is it regarded as a small miracle, since no one, anywhere, has ever successfully bred a flower and a tree before. It should not strictly have been possible, but his proofs are incontestable and the resulting plant is so beautiful that when it germinates they plant seedlings all around the campus, and Maciej notices a new measure of respect in the eyes of his teachers. A third year student, Hermann, goes out of his way to break ranks and congratulate Maciej on his achievement. His hand is warm and large as he pumps Maciej's arm and tells him, "At this rate, you will be famous before you even graduate."

"That isn't what I want," Maciej tells Hermann. "All is naught but for the Glory of God."

BY HIS SECOND year, Maciej is bored with most of his fellow students. They sit around the laboratories, dissecting cabbits and squittens that seem overly simplistic to Maciej. *Why would anyone try to genetically merge a cat and a rabbit,* he writes to Father Krzysztof, *let alone a squirrel? I fear many of my colleagues merely wish to create abominations: they foresee a world of square trees and seedless watermelons, acid-free tomatoes and strawberries reddened with genes from shrimp. The study of genetics could be so much more, could bring us closer to what we were in Eden. I feel so alone here.*

He keeps the letters Father Krzysztof sends him tucked inside his hardcover copy of *Lives of the Saints,* in the front cover of which he has pasted a periodic table of elements. He rereads these letters at night under the soft light of a sixty-watt bulb before he prays and consigns himself to sleep. *Loneliness is placed in the human heart by God, little Francis. St. Augustine said, "My soul will not rest, o Lord, until it rests in thee." Loneliness is what forces us to introduce ourselves to strangers, drives us outside of ourselves. It can lead to us to find love with our fellow human beings, a pale reflection of the love we have for God. Do not despise your loneliness, little Francis. It is a gift. And do not commit the sin of pride, thinking you are better than your colleagues. Make friends there. This Hermann you have mentioned seems to respect you and your work—seek out the good in him and turn a blind eye to the bad.*

From this point on, Maciej makes a point of taking meals with Hermann, talking to him in the afternoons and occasionally playing chess in the evenings. Hermann is the residence don on Maciej's floor, and it is considered an honour for a second-year to be invited to play chess in his don's room.

One night in spring, when the chess game is over, and the lights from the courtyard shine fluorescent into Hermann's room, the older boy breaks the silence of some minutes and asks Maciej what he is thinking.

"Of how to make a cow yield human milk," Maciej answers, "and how this could benefit mankind."

"Always with such heavy thoughts," Hermann says, reaching over to tousle his thin, mousy hair. "You should learn to lighten up."

"And I'm trying to isolate the gene for human kindness. Although I think that it must be a sequence rather than a single gene. But just think, Hermann! If I could increase people's genetic capacity for sympathy, empathy, kindness itself! Think of the increase in Christian charity I could bring into the world."

"If there is a gene for kindness, my friend, you definitely have it." With this he takes Maciej's hand and brings it to his rigid crotch. Maciej draws it back so fast a rush of air blows past his ears.

"Maciej, relax," Hermann whispers, laughing. "If you don't want to touch it, that's fine. But take yours out and let's have a pull together. I have some magazines hidden inside an old chemistry textbook." He grins.

"You should be ashamed," Maciej hisses. "Self-abuse is a terrible sin."

MACIEJ COMES HOME from class the next day, opens the door to his room and places his books on his desk. He feels unsettled, his skin has goosebumps and he can taste bile. He looks around his bare room wildly, trying to figure out what might make him feel so anxious. Finally he sees it; his mind catches on to what his physical senses had already noticed: his mother's crucifix, in its place above his bed, is hanging upside down. This takes his breath away. His left knee is shaking uncontrollably, his face grows cold and pale and prickles with sweat, until the spell breaks and he lunges up onto the bed and takes it off the wall. When he does, a small slip of paper falls down from behind it. In blue pen, in handwriting he recognizes, there is a message: *You should not have said no to me.* Maciej pockets the note and looks at the crucifix in his hand. He slows his breathing, thinks of his mother and Father Krzysztof, and says the Prayer Before a Crucifix in Polish and Latin. He puts the icon back in its place, right way up, and moves towards his textbooks with purpose.

MACIEJ'S REVENGE IS pre-emptive and swift. He thinks a week of stomach pain will make Hermann repent for his actions, suffer appropriately for his desecration. He extracts the venom of a Dugite snake, *Pseudonaja affinis,* the most poisonous snake in the laboratory, and he mixes it with the toxins of three different plants. His work is methodical, measured, as he toils under a single light until the rising sun illuminates his elixir with the soft golds and reds of dawn.

It is not difficult for him to mix his concoction with gravy, or pour it over food, not unusual for him to bring Hermann his lunch, all smiles as though nothing has happened. He says nothing when Hermann loses his appetite halfway through the meal, or when two other boys finish what Hermann has left.

Maciej is not, strictly speaking, a biologist. He has miscalculated, misjudged. By dusk the three boys are struck with a mysterious illness, not expected to live through the night. He does not come forward with any information about what he has done. He does not sleep, but prays for the three boys, and for forgiveness, all through the night, imagining his prayers carried on the feet of birds, large black ravens, circling higher and higher to Heaven. The three boys do not die that night, but the doctors say none of them will ever move a muscle again. They are taken away the next morning.

The Divinity Gene

THREE WEEKS LATER Maciej receives a letter from Father Benedykt telling him that Father Krzysztof has died. There is no money to bring Maciej back for the funeral. He is very sorry.

Maciej vomits when he reads the letter. He had sent no word since the night he spent making the poison. He was hoping to make a full confession the next time Father Krzysztof could visit, or he could get home. He turns on the cold-water faucet and lets the water pool in his hand, cups it to his mouth and rinses what he can't spit out. Everyone he has ever loved has left him. Why does God take all those who love him? Who will be proud of him now? What is he working for?

HE REREADS HIS letters from Father Krzysztof obsessively, neglecting his studies. He reads the priest's concerns about the foreign policies of Britain and America, the comparisons with Rome. He remembers the parish baptismal font, the adults converting at midnight Mass at Easter, the way the Joy of Christ's Light can brighten a face. He wishes he had ever seen a miracle. He wishes he could show miracles to others, the way a tree draws water from the ground, fifty feet into the air, the way a kidney purifies the blood. The perfect symmetry of a double helix.

He thinks about how he has been using science to try to help people, to help relieve temporal suffering during this life, to help reveal the Glory of God through the physical wonders of the world. But how much greater would it be to use science to reveal God directly, not through the medium of creation at all? Show people not merely the miracles that surround them in nature, but literal miracles like those in the pages of the Bible, enacted in their own lifetime? Show not merely the reflection of God, but His actual face made flesh? What then?

THE DIVINITY GENE

ACKNOWLEDGMENTS

"THORACIC EXAM" was previously published in *I.V. Lounge Nights* (Tightrope Books, 2008). My thanks to Alex Boyd for including me in the anthology.

"PAST PERFECT" won the Far Horizons Award for Short Fiction from the *Malahat Review* and appeared in issue 160. The contest asked writers to create stories from one of three sets of story notes found posthumously among Robin Skelton's papers. The prompt I used was as follows: "Sales Service: Garage sale. Buy Saturday sell Sunday. Then something occurs. Buy object (small statuette) sell Sunday, see it next Saturday, buy it, sell it. Price doesn't go up. Odd. Keep it a week... occurrences..." My thanks to John Barton for his sage editing of this story.

"iFAUST" appeared at www.forgetmagazine.com, volume 5, issue 2. My thanks to contributing editor Nick Thran.

"GUTTED" was previously published in *Matrix Magazine*, issue 83. My thanks to Jocelyn Parr and Jon Paul Fiorentino.

189

"CAMPING AT DEAD MAN'S POINT" was partially inspired by the story "Contaminant" in Ryan Boudinot's excellent collection, *The Littlest Hitler* (Counterpoint, 2006). The poem by Linda Besner mentioned in the story, entitled "Matthew J. Trafford," appeared in the anthologies *The Hoodoo You Do So Well* (Little Fishcart Press, 2007), *Rutting Season* (Buffalo Runs Press, 2009), and her own collection, *The Id Kid* (Véhicule Press, 2011).

"THE DIVINITY GENE" was previously published in *Darwin's Bastards: Astounding Tales from Tomorrow* (Douglas & McIntyre, 2010). My thanks to Chris Labonté and the inimitable Zsuzsi Gartner.

I ACKNOWLEDGE the support of the City of Toronto through the Toronto Arts Council (Writers Level One), as well as the Ontario Arts Council (Writers' Reserve and Writers' Works in Progress) and the Canada Council for the Arts (Creative Writing Program). This book would not have been possible without the support of programs such as these.

GRATITUDE

I would like to thank my parents for instilling in me a love of reading, and for supporting me unreservedly in my endeavours.

I am indebted to Zsuzsi Gartner—mentor, advocate, friend—for finding the short fiction writer inside of me and guiding many of these stories from their infancy to what they are today. Thank you.

Thanks to Edna Alford and Marilyn Bowering, who provided critical attention to drafts of these stories at the Banff Writing Studio. My work is much improved for your influence and close reading.

I thank my excellent editor, Barbara Berson, for her

patience, dedication, emotional insight, and keen analysis. I would also like to thank my copyeditor, Pam Robertson, for her accuracy, effort, and unflinching attention to the smallest and most important details.

I am incredibly grateful to the entire team at D&M who helped turn a file on my computer into a beautiful book out in the world. I am blessed to have such a talented, kind, and enthusiastic team working with me. My deepest thanks to Chris Labonté, for taking a second look and believing in me against the odds.

I owe a great deal to my teachers and classmates in the Optional-Residency Creative Writing MFA Program at the University of British Columbia, especially Andrew Gray, Sioux Browning, Sarah Selecky, Amy Jones, Cory Josephson, Adrienne Gruber, Diane Fleming, Tom Hansen, Paulette Bourgeois, Betty Jane Hegerat, and Stefan Riches. Most especially, I thank Laura Trunkey, my first reader, fellow warrior, and dear friend.

I want to express my appreciation to everyone who provided me with a quiet place to write: Catherine Wright and Greg Sacks, Teresa and Johnny Bourque, Sarah and Ryan Henderson, Dan McIlmoyl and Stef Seguin.

Thanks to those I live with, for their love and support during all of the madness: Jess Grant, Thomas Trafford, Meaghan George, and Adam Robinson. Thanks to Jane Henderson, Faduma Hashi, and Erin Deck, for keeping me sane. A special thank you to Linda Besner, who's believed in me and been writing by my side from the beginning.

Finally I would like to thank some people who passed from this life while I was writing the book, each of whom touched or supported me in some way: Dodie McNally, Gary Cameron, and Chris Lewis. Most profoundly of all, the Purv: M-O-O-N, that spells Mark Purvis. I miss you buddy.